A
ROOM *of*
one's OWN

Books by Virginia Woolf

The Voyage Out
Night and Day
Kew Gardens
Monday or Tuesday
Jacob's Room
The Common Reader: First Series
Mrs. Dalloway
To the Lighthouse
Orlando: A Biography
A Room of One's Own
The Waves
Letter to a Young Poet
The Common Reader: Second Series
Flush: A Biography
The Years
Three Guineas
Roger Fry: A Biography
Between the Acts
The Death of the Moth and Other Essays
A Haunted House and Other Short Stories
The Moment and Other Essays
The Captain's Death Bed and Other Essays
A Writer's Diary
Virginia Woolf and Lytton Strachey: Letters
Granite and Rainbow
Contemporary Writers
Collected Essays (*four volumes*)
Mrs. Dalloway's Party
The Letters of Virginia Woolf (*six volumes*)
Freshwater: A Comedy
Moments of Being
The Diary of Virginia Woolf (*five volumes*)
Books and Portraits
The Pargiters: The Novel-Essay Portion of *The Years*
Women and Writing
The Virginia Woolf Reader
The Common Reader: First Series Annotated Edition
The Complete Shorter Fiction of Virginia Woolf
The Common Reader: Second Series Annotated Edition
The Essays of Virginia Woolf, Vol. One (1904–1912)
The Widow and the Parrot
The Essays of Virginia Woolf, Vol. Two (1912–1918)
The Essays of Virginia Woolf, Vol. Three (1919–1924)
Congenial Spirits: The Selected Letters of Virginia Woolf
A Moment's Liberty: The Shorter Diary of Virginia Woolf
A Passionate Apprentice: The Early Journals, 1897–1909
Nurse Lugton's Curtain

A ROOM *of* *one's* OWN

VIRGINIA WOOLF

FALL
RIVER
PRESS

Fall River Press
122 Fifth Avenue
New York, NY 10011

ISBN-13: 978-0-7607-9183-7
ISBN-10: 0-7607-9183-X

Printed and bound in the United States of America

3 5 7 9 11 13 15 14 12 10 8 6 4 2

This essay is based upon two papers read to the Arts Society at Newnham and the Odtaa at Girton in October 1928. The papers were too long to be read in full, and have since been altered and expanded.

ONE

But, you may say, we asked you to speak about women and fiction—what has that got to do with a room of one's own? I will try to explain. When you asked me to speak about women and fiction I sat down on the banks of a river and began to wonder what the words meant. They might mean simply a few remarks about Fanny Burney; a few more about Jane Austen; a tribute to the Brontës and a sketch of Haworth Parsonage under snow; some witticisms if possible about Miss Mitford; a respectful allusion to George Eliot; a reference to Mrs. Gaskell and one would have done. But at second sight the words seemed not so simple. The title women and fiction might mean, and you may have meant it to mean, women and what they are like; or it might mean women and the fiction that they write; or it might mean women and the fiction that is written about them; or it might mean that somehow all three are inextricably mixed

I

together and you want me to consider them in that light. But when I began to consider the subject in this last way, which seemed the most interesting, I soon saw that it had one fatal drawback. I should never be able to come to a conclusion. I should never be able to fulfil what is, I understand, the first duty of a lecturer—to hand you after an hour's discourse a nugget of pure truth to wrap up between the pages of your notebooks and keep on the mantel-piece for ever. All I could do was to offer you an opinion upon one minor point—a woman must have money and a room of her own if she is to write fiction; and that, as you will see, leaves the great problem of the true nature of woman and the true nature of fiction unsolved. I have shirked the duty of coming to a conclusion upon these two questions—women and fiction remain, so far as I am concerned, unsolved problems. But in order to make some amends I am going to do what I can to show you how I arrived at this opinion about the room and the money. I am going to develop in your presence as fully and freely as I can the train of thought which led me to think this. Perhaps if I lay bare the ideas, the prejudices, that lie behind this statement you will find that they have some bearing upon women and some upon fiction. At any rate, when a subject is highly controversial—and any question about sex is that—one cannot hope to tell the truth. One can only show how one came to hold whatever opinion one does hold. One can only give one's audience the chance of drawing their own conclusions as they observe the limitations, the prejudices, the idiosyncrasies of the speaker. Fiction here is likely to contain more truth than fact. Therefore I propose, making use of all the liberties and licences of a novelist, to tell you the story of the two days that preceded my coming here—how, bowed down by the weight of the subject which you have laid upon my shoulders, I pondered it, and made it work in and out of my daily life. I need not say that what I am about to describe has no existence; Oxbridge is an invention; so is Fernham; "I" is only a convenient term for somebody who has no real being. Lies will flow from my lips, but there may perhaps be some truth mixed up with them; it is for you to seek out this truth and to decide whether any part of it is worth keeping. If not, you will of course throw the whole of it into the wastepaper basket and forget all about it.

Here then was I (call me Mary Beton, Mary Seton, Mary Carmichael or by any name you please—it is not a matter of any importance) sitting on the banks of a river a week or two ago in fine October weather, lost in thought. That collar I have spoken of, women and fiction, the need of coming to some conclusion on a subject that raises all sorts of prejudices and passions, bowed my head to the ground. To the right and left bushes of some sort, golden and crimson, glowed with the colour, even it seemed burnt with the heat, of fire. On the further bank the willows wept in perpetual lamentation, their hair about their shoulders. The river reflected whatever it chose of sky and bridge and burning tree, and when the undergraduate had oared his boat through the reflections they closed again, completely, as if he had never been. There one might have sat the clock round lost in thought. Thought—to call it by a prouder name than it deserved—had let its line down into the stream. It swayed, minute after minute, hither and thither among the reflections and the weeds, letting the water lift it and sink it, until—you know the little tug—the sudden conglomeration of an idea at the end of one's line: and then the cautious hauling of it in, and the careful laying of it out? Alas, laid on the grass how small, how insignificant this thought of mine looked; the sort of fish that a good fisherman puts back into the water so that it may grow fatter and be one day worth cooking and eating. I will not trouble you with that thought now, though if you look carefully you may find it for yourselves in the course of what I am going to say.

But however small it was, it had, nevertheless, the mysterious property of its kind—put back into the mind, it became at once very exciting, and important; and as it darted and sank, and flashed hither and thither, set up such a wash and tumult of ideas that it was impossible to sit still. It was thus that I found myself walking with extreme rapidity across a grass plot. Instantly a man's figure rose to intercept me. Nor did I at first understand that the gesticulations of a curious-looking object, in a cut-away coat and evening shirt, were aimed at me. His face expressed horror and indignation. Instinct rather than reason came to my help; he was a Beadle; I was a woman. This was the turf; there was the path. Only the Fellows and Scholars are allowed here; the gravel is the place for me. Such thoughts were the work of a moment. As I regained the path the arms of the Beadle sank, his face assumed its usual repose, and though turf is better walking than gravel, no very great harm was done. The only charge I could bring against the Fellows and Scholars of whatever the college might happen to be was that in protection of their turf, which has been rolled for 300 years in succession, they had sent my little fish into hiding.

What idea it had been that had sent me so audaciously

trespassing I could not now remember. The spirit of peace descended like a cloud from heaven, for if the spirit of peace dwells anywhere, it is in the courts and quadrangles of Oxbridge on a fine October morning. Strolling through those colleges past those ancient halls the roughness of the present seemed smoothed away; the body seemed contained in a miraculous glass cabinet through which no sound could penetrate, and the mind, freed from any contact with facts (unless one trespassed on the turf again), was at liberty to settle down upon whatever meditation was in harmony with the moment. As chance would have it, some stray memory of some old essay about revisiting Oxbridge in the long vacation brought Charles Lamb to mind—Saint Charles, said Thackeray, putting a letter of Lamb's to his forehead. Indeed, among all the dead (I give you my thoughts as they came to me), Lamb is one of the most congenial; one to whom one would have liked to say, Tell me then how you wrote your essays? For his essays are superior even to Max Beerbohm's, I thought, with all their perfection, because of that wild flash of imagination, that lightning crack of genius in the middle of them which leaves them flawed and imperfect, but starred with poetry. Lamb then came to Oxbridge perhaps a hundred years ago. Certainly he wrote an essay—the name escapes me—about the manuscript of one of Milton's poems which he saw here. It was *Lycidas* perhaps, and Lamb wrote how it shocked him to think it possible that any word in *Lycidas* could have been different from what it is. To think of Milton changing the words in that poem seemed to him a sort of sacrilege. This led me to remember what I could of *Lycidas* and to amuse myself with guessing which word it could have been that Milton had altered, and why. It then occurred to me that the very manuscript itself which Lamb had looked at was only a few hundred yards away, so that one could follow Lamb's footsteps across the quadrangle to that famous library where the treasure is kept. Moreover, I recollected, as I put this plan into execution, it is in this famous library that the manuscript of Thackeray's *Esmond* is also preserved. The critics often say that *Esmond* is Thackeray's most perfect novel. But the affectation of the style, with its imitation of the eighteenth century, hampers one, so far as I remember; unless indeed the eighteenth-century style was natural to Thackeray—a fact that one might prove by looking at the manuscript and seeing whether the alterations were for the benefit of the style or of the sense. But then one would have to decide what is style and what is meaning, a question which—but here I was actually at the door which leads into the library itself. I must have opened it, for instantly there issued, like a guardian angel barring the way with a flutter of black gown instead of white wings, a deprecating, silvery, kindly gentleman, who regretted in a low voice as he waved me back that ladies are only admitted to the library if accompanied by a Fellow of the College or furnished with a letter of introduction.

That a famous library has been cursed by a woman is a matter of complete indifference to a famous library. Venerable and calm, with all its treasures safe locked within its breast, it sleeps complacently and will, so far as I am concerned, so sleep for ever. Never will I wake those echoes, never will I ask for that hospitality again, I vowed as I descended the steps in anger. Still an hour remained before luncheon, and what was one to do? Stroll on the meadows? sit by the river? Certainly it was a lovely autumn morning; the leaves were fluttering red to the ground; there was no great hardship in doing either. But the sound of music reached my ear. Some service or celebration was going forward. The organ complained magnificently as I passed the chapel door. Even the sorrow of Christianity sounded in that serene air more like the recollection of sorrow than sorrow itself; even the groanings of the ancient organ seemed lapped in peace. I had no wish to enter had I the right, and this time the verger might have stopped me, demanding perhaps my baptismal certificate, or a letter of introduction from the Dean. But the outside of these magnificent buildings is often as beautiful as the inside. Moreover, it was amusing enough to watch the congregation assembling, coming in and going out again, busying themselves at the door of the chapel like bees at the mouth of a hive. Many were in cap and gown; some had tufts of fur on their shoulders; others were wheeled in bath-chairs; others, though not past middle age, seemed creased and crushed into shapes so singular that one was reminded of those giant crabs and crayfish who heave with difficulty across the sand of an aquarium. As I leant against the wall the University indeed seemed a sanctuary in which are preserved rare types which would soon be obsolete if left to fight for existence on the pavement of the Strand. Old stories of old deans and old dons came back to mind, but before I had summoned up courage to whistle—it used to be said that at the sound of a whistle old Professor _____ instantly broke into a gallop—the venerable congregation had gone inside. The outside of the chapel remained. As you know, its high domes and pinnacles can be seen, like a sailing-ship always voyaging never arriving, lit up at night and visible for miles, far away across the hills. Once, presumably, this quadrangle with its smooth lawns, its massive buildings, and the chapel itself was marsh too, where the grasses waved and the swine rootled. Teams of horses and oxen, I thought, must have hauled the stone in wagons from far countries, and then with infinite labour the grey blocks in whose shade I was now standing were poised in order one on top of another, and then the painters brought their glass for the windows, and the masons were busy for centuries up on that roof with putty and cement, spade and trowel. Every Saturday somebody must have poured gold and silver out of a leathern purse into their ancient fists, for they had their beer and skittles presumably of an evening. An unending stream of gold and silver, I thought, must have flowed into this court perpetually to keep the stones coming and the masons working; to level, to ditch, to dig and to drain. But it was then the age of faith, and money was poured liberally to set these stones on a deep foundation, and when the stones were raised, still more money was poured in from the coffers of kings and queens and great nobles to ensure that hymns should be sung here and scholars taught. Lands were granted; tithes were paid. And when the age of faith was over and the age of reason had come, still the same flow of gold and silver went on; fellowships were founded; lectureships endowed; only the gold and silver flowed now, not from the coffers of the king, but from the chests of merchants and manufacturers, from the purses of men who had made, say, a fortune from industry, and returned, in their wills, a bounteous share of it to endow more chairs, more lectureships, more fellowships in the university where they had learnt their craft. Hence the libraries and laboratories; the observatories; the splendid equipment of costly and delicate instruments which now stands on glass shelves, where centuries ago the grasses waved and the swine rootled. Certainly, as I strolled round the court, the foundation of gold and silver seemed deep enough; the pavement laid solidly over the wild grasses. Men with trays on their heads went busily from staircase to staircase. Gaudy blossoms flowered in window-boxes. The strains of the gramophone blared out from the rooms within. It was impossible not to reflect—the reflection whatever it may have been was cut short. The clock struck. It was time to find one's way to luncheon.

It is a curious fact that novelists have a way of making us believe that luncheon parties are invariably memorable for something very witty that was said, or for something very wise that was done. But they seldom spare a word for what was eaten. It is part of the novelist's convention not to mention soup and salmon and ducklings, as if soup and salmon and ducklings were of no importance whatsoever, as if nobody ever smoked a cigar or drank a glass of wine. Here, however, I shall take the liberty to defy that convention and to tell you that the lunch on this occasion began with soles, sunk in a deep dish, over which the college cook had spread a counterpane of the whitest cream, save that it was branded here and there with brown spots like the spots on the flanks of a doe. After that came the partridges, but if this suggests a couple of bald, brown birds on a plate you are mistaken. The partridges, many and various, came with all their retinue of sauces and salads, the sharp and the sweet, each in its order; their potatoes, thin as coins but not so hard; their sprouts, foliated as rosebuds but more succulent. And no sooner had the roast and its retinue been done with than the silent serving-man, the Beadle himself perhaps in a milder manifestation, set before us, wreathed in napkins, a confection which rose all sugar from the waves. To call it pudding and so relate it to rice and tapioca would be an insult. Meanwhile the wine-glasses had flushed yellow and flushed crimson; had been emptied; had been filled. And thus by degrees was lit, halfway down the spine, which is the seat of the soul, not that hard little electric light which we call brilliance, as it pops in and out upon our lips, but the more profound, subtle and subterranean glow, which is the rich yellow flame of rational intercourse. No need to hurry. No need to sparkle. No need to be anybody but oneself. We are all going to heaven and Vandyck is of the company—in other words, how good life seemed, how sweet its rewards, how trivial this grudge or that grievance, how admirable friendship and the society of one's kind, as, lighting a good cigarette, one sunk among the cushions in the window-seat.

If by good luck there had been an ash-tray handy, if one had not knocked the ash out of the window in default, if things had been a little different from what they were, one would not have seen, presumably, a cat without a tail. The sight of that abrupt and truncated animal padding softly across the quadrangle changed by some fluke of the subconscious intelligence the emotional light for me. It was as if some one had let fall a shade. Perhaps the excellent hock was relinquishing its hold. Certainly, as I watched the Manx cat pause in the middle of the lawn as if it too questioned the universe, something seemed lacking, something seemed different. But what was lacking, what was different, I asked myself, listening to the talk. And to answer that question I had to think myself out of the room, back into the past, before the war indeed, and to set before my eyes the model of another luncheon party held in rooms not very far distant from these; but different. Everything was different. Meanwhile the talk went on among the guests, who were many and young, some of this sex, some of that; it went on swimmingly, it went on agreeably, freely, amusingly. And as it went on I set it against the background of that other talk, and as I matched the two together I had no doubt that one was the descendant, the legitimate heir of the other. Nothing was changed; nothing was different save only—here I listened with all my ears not entirely to what was being said, but to the murmur or current behind it. Yes, that was it—the change was there. Before the war at a luncheon party like this people would have said precisely the same things but they would have sounded different, because in those days they were accompanied by a sort of humming noise, not articulate, but musical, exciting, which changed the value of the words themselves. Could one set that humming noise to words? Perhaps with the help of the poets one could. A book lay beside me and, opening it, I turned casually enough to Tennyson. And here I found Tennyson was singing:

> *There has fallen a splendid tear*
> *From the passion-flower at the gate.*
> *She is coming, my dove, my dear;*
> *She is coming, my life, my fate;*
> *The red rose cries, "She is near, she is near";*
> *And the white rose weeps, "She is late";*
> *The larkspur listens, "I hear, I hear";*
> *And the lily whispers, "I wait."*

Was that what men hummed at luncheon parties before the war? And the women?

> *My heart is like a singing bird*
>   *Whose nest is in a water'd shoot;*
> *My heart is like an apple tree*
>   *Whose boughs are bent with thick-set fruit;*
> *My heart is like a rainbow shell*
>   *That paddles in a halcyon sea;*
> *My heart is gladder than all these*
>   *Because my love is come to me.*

Was that what women hummed at luncheon parties before the war?

There was something so ludicrous in thinking of people humming such things even under their breath at luncheon parties before the war that I burst out laughing, and had to explain my laughter by pointing at the Manx cat, who did look a little absurd, poor beast, without a tail, in the middle of the lawn. Was he really born so, or had he lost his tail in an accident? The tailless cat, though some are said to exist in the Isle of Man, is rarer than one thinks. It is a queer animal, quaint rather than beautiful. It is strange what a difference a tail makes— you know the sort of things one says as a lunch party breaks up and people are finding their coats and hats.

This one, thanks to the hospitality of the host, had lasted far into the afternoon. The beautiful October day was fading and the leaves were falling from the trees in the avenue as I walked through it. Gate after gate seemed to close with gentle finality behind me. Innumerable beadles were fitting innumerable keys into well-oiled locks; the treasure-house was being made secure for another night. After the avenue one comes out upon a road—I forget its name—which leads you, if you take the right turning, along to Fernham. But there was plenty of time. Dinner was not till half-past seven. One could almost do without dinner after such a luncheon. It is strange how a scrap of poetry works in the mind and makes the legs move in time to it along the road. Those words—

> *There has fallen a splendid tear*
> *From the passion-flower at the gate.*
> *She is coming, my dove, my dear—*

sang in my blood as I stepped quickly along towards Headingley. And then, switching off into the other measure, I sang, where the waters are churned up by the weir:

> *My heart is like a singing bird*
> *Whose nest is in a water'd shoot;*
> *My heart is like an apple tree . . .*

What poets, I cried aloud, as one does in the dusk, what poets they were!

In a sort of jealousy, I suppose, for our own age, silly and absurd though these comparisons are, I went on to wonder if honestly one could name two living poets now as great as Tennyson and Christina Rossetti were then. Obviously it is impossible, I thought, looking into those foaming waters, to compare them. The very reason why the poetry excites one to such abandonment, such rapture, is that it celebrates some feeling that one used to have (at luncheon parties before the war perhaps), so that one responds easily, familiarly, without troubling to check the feeling, or to compare it with any that one has now. But the living poets express a feeling that is actually being made and torn out of us at the moment. One does not recognize it in the first place; often for some reason one fears it; one watches it with keenness and compares it jealously and suspiciously with the old feeling that one knew. Hence the difficulty of modern poetry; and it is because of this difficulty that one cannot remember more than two consecutive lines of any good modern poet. For this reason—that my memory failed me—the argument flagged for want of material. But why, I continued, moving on towards Headingley, have we stopped humming under our breath at luncheon parties? Why has Alfred ceased to sing

She is coming, my dove, my dear?

Why has Christina ceased to respond

My heart is gladder than all these
Because my love is come to me?

Shall we lay the blame on the war? When the guns fired in August 1914, did the faces of men and women show so plain in each other's eyes that romance was killed? Certainly it was a shock (to women in particular with their illusions about education, and so on) to see the faces of our rulers in the light of the shell-fire. So ugly they looked—German, English, French—so stupid. But lay the blame where one will, on whom one will, the illusion which inspired Tennyson and Christina Rossetti to sing so passionately about the coming of their loves is far rarer now than then. One has only to read, to look, to listen, to remember. But why say "blame"? Why, if it was an illusion, not praise the catastrophe, whatever it was, that destroyed illusion and put truth in its place? For truth . . . those dots mark the spot where, in search of truth, I missed the turning up to Fernham. Yes indeed, which was truth and which was illusion, I asked myself. What was the truth about these houses, for example, dim and festive now with their red windows in the dusk, but raw and red and squalid, with their sweets and their boot-laces, at nine o'clock in the morning? And the willows and the river and the gardens that run down to the river, vague now with the mist stealing over them, but gold and red in the sunlight—which was the truth, which was the illusion about them? I spare you the twists and turns of my cogitations, for no conclusion was found on the road to Headingley, and I ask you to suppose that I soon found out my mistake about the turning and retraced my steps to Fernham.

As I have said already that it was an October day, I dare not forfeit your respect and imperil the fair name of fiction by changing the season and describing lilacs hanging over garden walls, crocuses, tulips and other flowers of spring. Fiction must stick to facts, and the truer the facts the better the fiction—so we are told. Therefore it was still autumn and the leaves were still yellow and falling, if anything, a little faster than before, because it was now evening (seven twenty-three to be precise) and a breeze (from the southwest to be exact) had risen. But for all that there was something odd at work:

My heart is like a singing bird
  Whose nest is in a water'd shoot;
My heart is like an apple tree
  Whose boughs are bent with thick-set fruit—

perhaps the words of Christina Rossetti were partly responsible for the folly of the fancy—it was nothing of course but a fancy—that the lilac was shaking its flowers over the garden walls, and the brimstone butterflies were scudding hither and thither, and the dust of the pollen was in the air. A wind blew, from what quarter I know not, but it lifted the half-grown leaves so that there was a flash of silver grey in the air. It was the time between the lights when colours undergo their intensification and purples and golds burn in window-panes like the beat of an excitable heart; when for some reason the beauty of the world revealed and yet soon to perish (here I pushed into the garden, for, unwisely, the door was left open and no beadles seemed about), the beauty of the world which is soon to perish, has two edges, one of laughter, one of anguish, cutting the heart asunder. The gardens of Fernham lay before me in the spring twilight, wild and open, and in the long grass, sprinkled and carelessly flung, were daffodils and bluebells, not orderly perhaps at the best of times, and now wind-blown and waving as they tugged at their roots. The windows of the building, curved like ships' windows among generous waves of red brick, changed from lemon to silver under the flight of the quick spring clouds. Somebody was in a hammock, somebody, but in this light they were phantoms only, half guessed, half seen, raced across the grass—would no one stop her?—and then on the terrace, as if popping out to breathe the air, to glance at the garden, came a bent figure, formidable yet humble, with her great forehead and her shabby dress—could it be the famous scholar, could it be J____ H____ herself? All was dim, yet intense too, as if the scarf which the dusk had flung over the garden were torn asunder by star or sword—the flash of some terrible reality leaping, as its way is, out of the heart of the spring. For youth——

Here was my soup. Dinner was being served in the great dining-hall. Far from being spring it was in fact an evening in October. Everybody was assembled in the big dining-room. Dinner was ready. Here was the soup. It was a plain gravy soup. There was nothing to stir the fancy in that. One could have seen through the transparent liquid any pattern that there might have been on the plate itself. But there was no pattern. The plate was plain. Next came beef with its attendant greens and potatoes—a homely trinity, suggesting the rumps of cattle in a muddy market, and sprouts curled and yellowed at the edge, and bargaining and cheapening, and women with string bags on Monday morning. There was no reason to complain of human nature's daily food, seeing that the supply was sufficient and coal-miners doubtless were sitting down to less. Prunes and custard followed. And if any one complains that prunes, even when mitigated by custard, are an uncharitable vegetable (fruit they are not), stringy as a miser's heart and exuding a fluid such as might run in misers' veins who have denied themselves wine and warmth for eighty years and yet not given to the poor, he should reflect that there are people whose charity embraces even the prune. Biscuits and cheese came next, and here the water-jug was liberally passed round, for it is the nature of biscuits to be dry, and these were biscuits to the core. That was all.

The meal was over. Everybody scraped their chairs back; the swing-doors swung violently to and fro; soon the hall was emptied of every sign of food and made ready no doubt for breakfast next morning. Down corridors and up staircases the youth of England went banging and singing. And was it for a guest, a stranger (for I had no more right here in Fernham than in Trinity or Somerville or Girton or Newnham or Christchurch), to say, "The dinner was not good," or to say (we were now, Mary Seton and I, in her sitting-room), "Could we not have dined up here alone?" for if I had said anything of the kind I should have been prying and searching into the secret economies of a house which to the stranger wears so fine a front of gaiety and courage. No, one could say nothing of the sort. Indeed, conversation for a moment flagged. The human frame being what it is, heart, body and brain all mixed together, and not contained in separate compartments as they will be no doubt in another million years, a good dinner is of great importance to good talk. One cannot think well, love well, sleep well, if one has not dined well. The lamp in the spine does not light on beef and prunes. We are all *probably* going to heaven, and Vandyck is, we *hope*, to meet us round the next corner—that is the dubious and qualifying state of mind that beef and prunes at the end of the day's work breed between them. Happily my friend, who taught science, had a cupboard where there was a squat bottle and little glasses—(but there should have been sole and partridge to begin with)—so that we were able to draw up to the fire and repair some of the damages of the day's living. In a minute or so we were slipping freely in and out among all those objects of curiosity and interest which form in the mind in the absence of a particular person, and are naturally to be discussed on coming together again—how somebody has married, another has not; one thinks this, another that; one has improved out of all knowledge, the other most amazingly gone to the bad—with all those speculations upon human nature and the character of the amazing world we live in which spring naturally from such beginnings. While these things were being said, however, I became shamefacedly aware of a current setting in of its own accord and carrying everything forward to an end of its own. One might be talking of Spain or Portugal, of book or racehorse, but the real interest of whatever was said was none of those things, but a scene of masons on a high roof some five centuries ago. Kings and nobles brought treasure in huge sacks and poured it under the earth. This scene was for ever coming alive in my mind and placing itself by another of lean cows and a muddy market and withered greens and the stringy hearts of old men—these two pictures, disjointed and disconnected and nonsensical as they were, were for ever coming together and combating each other and had me entirely at their mercy. The best course, unless the whole talk was to be distorted, was to expose what was in my mind to the air, when with good luck it would fade and crumble like the head of the dead king when they opened the coffin at Windsor. Briefly, then, I told Miss Seton about the masons who had been all those years on the roof of the chapel, and about the kings and queens and nobles bearing sacks of gold and silver on their shoulders, which they shovelled into the earth; and then how the great financial magnates of our own time came and laid

VIRGINIA WOOLF

cheques and bonds, I suppose, where the others had laid
ingots and rough lumps of gold. All that lies beneath the
colleges down there, I said; but this college, where we
are now sitting, what lies beneath its gallant red brick
and the wild unkempt grasses of the garden? What force
is behind the plain china off which we dined, and (here
it popped out of my mouth before I could stop it) the
beef, the custard and the prunes?

Well, said Mary Seton, about the year 1860—Oh, but
you know the story, she said, bored, I suppose, by the
recital. And she told me—rooms were hired. Commit-
tees met. Envelopes were addressed. Circulars were
drawn up. Meetings were held; letters were read out;
so-and-so has promised so much; on the contrary,
Mr. ____ won't give a penny. The *Saturday Review* has
been very rude. How can we raise a fund to pay for
offices? Shall we hold a bazaar? Can't we find a pretty
girl to sit in the front row? Let us look up what John
Stuart Mill said on the subject. Can any one persuade
the editor of the ____ to print a letter? Can we get
Lady ____ to sign it? Lady ____ is out of town. That
was the way it was done, presumably, sixty years ago,
and it was a prodigious effort, and a great deal of time
was spent on it. And it was only after a long struggle
and with the utmost difficulty that they got thirty thousand pounds together.[1] So obviously we cannot have
wine and partridges and servants carrying tin dishes on
their heads, she said. We cannot have sofas and separate

1 "We are told that we ought to ask for £30,000 at least. . . . It is not a large
sum, considering that there is to be but one college of this sort for Great
Britain, Ireland and the Colonies, and considering how easy it is to raise
immense sums for boys' schools. But considering how few people really wish
women to be educated, it is a good deal."—LADY STEPHEN, *Life of Miss
Emily Davies*.

rooms. "The amenities," she said, quoting from some book or other, "will have to wait."[1]

At the thought of all those women working year after year and finding it hard to get two thousand pounds together, and as much as they could do to get thirty thousand pounds, we burst out in scorn at the reprehensible poverty of our sex. What had our mothers been doing then that they had no wealth to leave us? Powdering their noses? Looking in at shop windows? Flaunting in the sun at Monte Carlo? There were some photographs on the mantel-piece. Mary's mother—if that was her picture—may have been a wastrel in her spare time (she had thirteen children by a minister of the church), but if so her gay and dissipated life had left too few traces of its pleasures on her face. She was a homely body; an old lady in a plaid shawl which was fastened by a large cameo; and she sat in a basket-chair, encouraging a spaniel to look at the camera, with the amused, yet strained expression of one who is sure that the dog will move directly the bulb is pressed. Now if she had gone into business; had become a manufacturer of artificial silk or a magnate on the Stock Exchange; if she had left two or three hundred thousand pounds to Fernham, we could have been sitting at our ease tonight and the subject of our talk might have been archaeology, botany, anthropology, physics, the nature of the atom, mathematics, astronomy, relativity, geography. If only Mrs. Seton and her mother and her mother before her had learnt the great art of making money and had left their money, like their fathers and their grandfathers before them, to found fellowships and lectureships and

1 Every penny which could be scraped together was set aside for building, and the amenities had to be postponed.—R. STRACHEY, *The Cause.*

prizes and scholarships appropriated to the use of their own sex, we might have dined very tolerably up here alone off a bird and a bottle of wine; we might have looked forward without undue confidence to a pleasant and honourable lifetime spent in the shelter of one of the liberally endowed professions. We might have been exploring or writing; mooning about the venerable places of the earth; sitting contemplative on the steps of the Parthenon, or going at ten to an office and coming home comfortably at half-past four to write a little poetry. Only, if Mrs. Seton and her like had gone into business at the age of fifteen, there would have been—that was the snag in the argument—no Mary. What, I asked, did Mary think of that? There between the curtains was the October night, calm and lovely, with a star or two caught in the yellowing trees. Was she ready to resign her share of it and her memories (for they had been a happy family, though a large one) of games and quarrels up in Scotland, which she is never tired of praising for the fineness of its air and the quality of its cakes, in order that Fernham might have been endowed with fifty thousand pounds or so by a stroke of the pen? For, to endow a college would necessitate the suppression of families altogether. Making a fortune and bearing thirteen children—no human being could stand it. Consider the facts, we said. First there are nine months before the baby is born. Then the baby is born. Then there are three or four months spent in feeding the baby. After the baby is fed there are certainly five years spent in playing with the baby. You cannot, it seems, let children run about the streets. People who have seen them running wild in Russia say that the sight is not a pleasant one. People say, too, that human nature takes its shape in the years between one and five. If Mrs. Seton, I said, had been making money, what sort of memories would you have had of games and quarrels? What would you have known of Scotland, and its fine air and cakes and all the rest of it? But it is useless to ask these questions, because you would never have come into existence at all. Moreover, it is equally useless to ask what might have happened if Mrs. Seton and her mother and her mother before her had amassed great wealth and laid it under the foundations of college and library, because, in the first place, to earn money was impossible for them, and in the second, had it been possible, the law denied them the right to possess what money they earned. It is only for the last forty-eight years that Mrs. Seton has had a penny of her own. For all the centuries before that it would have been her husband's property—a thought which, perhaps, may have had its share in keeping Mrs. Seton and her mothers off the Stock Exchange. Every penny I earn, they may have said, will be taken from me and disposed of according to my husband's wisdom—perhaps to found a scholarship or to endow a fellowship in Balliol or Kings, so that to earn money, even if I could earn money, is not a matter that interests me very greatly. I had better leave it to my husband.

At any rate, whether or not the blame rested on the old lady who was looking at the spaniel, there could be no doubt that for some reason or other our mothers had mismanaged their affairs very gravely. Not a penny could be spared for "amenities"; for partridges and wine, beadles and turf, books and cigars, libraries and leisure. To raise bare walls out of the bare earth was the utmost they could do.

So we talked standing at the window and looking, as

so many thousands look every night, down on the domes and towers of the famous city beneath us. It was very beautiful, very mysterious in the autumn moonlight. The old stone looked very white and venerable. One thought of all the books that were assembled down there; of the pictures of old prelates and worthies hanging in the panelled rooms; of the painted windows that would be throwing strange globes and crescents on the pavement; of the tablets and memorials and inscriptions; of the fountains and the grass; of the quiet rooms looking across the quiet quadrangles. And (pardon me the thought) I thought, too, of the admirable smoke and drink and the deep armchairs and the pleasant carpets: of the urbanity, the geniality, the dignity which are the offspring of luxury and privacy and space. Certainly our mothers had not provided us with anything comparable to all this— our mothers who found it difficult to scrape together thirty thousand pounds, our mothers who bore thirteen children to ministers of religion at St. Andrews.

So I went back to my inn, and as I walked through the dark streets I pondered this and that, as one does at the end of the day's work. I pondered why it was that Mrs. Seton had no money to leave us; and what effect poverty has on the mind; and what effect wealth has on the mind; and I thought of the queer old gentlemen I had seen that morning with tufts of fur upon their shoulders; and I remembered how if one whistled one of them ran; and I thought of the organ booming in the chapel and of the shut doors of the library; and I thought how unpleasant it is to be locked out; and I thought how it is worse perhaps to be locked in; and, thinking of the safety and prosperity of the one sex and of the poverty and insecurity of the other and of the effect of tradition and of the lack of tradition upon the mind of a writer, I thought at last that it was time to roll up the crumpled skin of the day, with its arguments and its impressions and its anger and its laughter, and cast it into the hedge. A thousand stars were flashing across the blue wastes of the sky. One seemed alone with an inscrutable society. All human beings were laid asleep—prone, horizontal, dumb. Nobody seemed stirring in the streets of Oxbridge. Even the door of the hotel sprang open at the touch of an invisible hand—not a boots was sitting up to light me to bed, it was so late.

Two

The scene, if I may ask you to follow me, was now changed. The leaves were still falling, but in London now, not Oxbridge; and I must ask you to imagine a room, like many thousands, with a window looking across people's hats and vans and motor-cars to other windows, and on the table inside the room a blank sheet of paper on which was written in large letters WOMEN AND FICTION, but no more. The inevitable sequel to lunching and dining at Oxbridge seemed, unfortunately, to be a visit to the British Museum. One must strain off what was personal and accidental in all these impressions and so reach the pure fluid, the essential oil of truth. For that visit to Oxbridge and the luncheon and the dinner had started a swarm of questions. Why did men drink wine and women water? Why was one sex so prosperous and the other so poor? What effect has poverty on fiction? What conditions are necessary for the creation of works of art?—a thousand questions at once suggested themselves. But one needed answers, not questions; and an answer was only to be had by consulting the learned and the unprejudiced, who have removed themselves above the strife of tongue and the confusion of body and issued the result of their reasoning and research in books which are to be found in the British Museum. If truth is not to be found on the shelves of the British Museum, where, I asked myself, picking up a notebook and a pencil, is truth?

Thus provided, thus confident and enquiring, I set out in the pursuit of truth. The day, though not actually wet, was dismal, and the streets in the neighborhood of the Museum were full of open coal-holes, down which sacks were showering; four-wheeled cabs were drawing up and depositing on the pavement corded boxes containing, presumably, the entire wardrobe of some Swiss or Italian family seeking fortune or refuge or some other desirable commodity which is to be found in the boarding-houses of Bloomsbury in the winter. The usual hoarse-voiced men paraded the streets with plants on barrows. Some shouted; others sang. London was like a workshop. London was like a machine. We were all being shot backwards and forwards on this plain foundation to make some pattern. The British Museum was another department of the factory. The swing-doors swung open; and there one stood under the vast dome, as if one were a thought in the huge bald forehead which is so splendidly encircled by a band of famous names. One went to the counter; one took a slip of paper; one opened a volume of the catalogue, and . . . . . the five dots here indicate five separate minutes of stupefaction, wonder and bewilderment. Have you any notion how many books are written about women in the course of one year? Have you any notion how many are written by men? Are you aware that you are, perhaps, the most discussed animal in the universe? Here had I come with a notebook and a pencil proposing to spend a morning reading, supposing that at the end of the morning I should have transferred the truth to my notebook. But I should need to be a herd of elephants, I thought, and a wilderness of spiders, desperately referring to the animals that are reputed longest lived and most multitudinously eyed, to cope with all this. I should need claws of steel and beak of brass even to penetrate the husk. How shall I ever find the grains of truth embedded in all this mass of paper, I asked myself, and in despair began running my eye up and down the long list of titles. Even the names of the books gave me food for thought. Sex and its nature might well attract doctors and biologists; but what was surprising and difficult of explanation was the fact that sex—woman, that is to say— also attracts agreeable essayists, light-fingered novelists, young men who have taken the M.A. degree; men who have taken no degree; men who have no apparent qualification save that they are not women. Some of these books were, on the face of it, frivolous and facetious; but many, on the other hand, were serious and prophetic, moral and hortatory. Merely to read the titles suggested innumerable schoolmasters, innumerable clergymen mounting their platforms and pulpits and holding forth with a loquacity which far exceeded the hour usually allotted to such discourse on this one subject. It was a most strange phenomenon; and apparently—here I consulted the letter M—one confined to male sex. Women do not write books about men—a fact that I

28

could not help welcoming with relief, for if I had first to read all that men have written about women, then all that women have written about men, the aloe that flowers once in a hundred years would flower twice before I could set pen to paper. So, making a perfectly arbitrary choice of a dozen volumes or so, I sent my slips of paper to lie in the wire tray, and waited in my stall, among the other seekers for the essential oil of truth.

What could be the reason, then, of this curious disparity, I wondered, drawing cart-wheels on the slips of paper provided by the British taxpayer for other purposes. Why are women, judging from this catalogue, so much more interesting to men than men are to women? A very curious fact it seemed, and my mind wandered to picture the lives of men who spend their time in writing books about women; whether they were old or young, married or unmarried, red-nosed or humpbacked—anyhow, it was flattering, vaguely, to feel oneself the object of such attention, provided that it was not entirely bestowed by the crippled and the infirm—so I pondered until all such frivolous thoughts were ended by an avalanche of books sliding down on to the desk in front of me. Now the trouble began. The student who has been trained in research at Oxbridge has no doubt some method of shepherding his question past all distractions till it runs into its answer as a sheep runs into its pen. The student by my side, for instance, who was copying assiduously from a scientific manual was, I felt sure, extracting pure nuggets of the essential ore every ten minutes or so. His little grunts of satisfaction indicated so much. But if, unfortunately, one has had no training in a university, the question far from being shepherded to its pen flies like a frightened flock hither and thither, helter-skelter, pursued by a whole pack of hounds. Professors, schoolmasters, sociologists, clergymen, novelists, essayists, journalists, men who had no qualification save that they were not women, chased my simple and single question—Why are women poor?—until it became fifty questions; until the fifty questions leapt frantically into mid-stream and were carried away. Every page in my notebook was scribbled over with notes. To show the state of mind I was in, I will read you a few of them, explaining that the page was headed quite simply, WOMEN AND POVERTY, in block letters; but what followed was something like this:

Condition in Middle Ages of,
Habits in the Fiji Islands of,
Worshipped as goddesses by,
Weaker in moral sense than,
Idealism of,
Greater conscientiousness of,
South Sea Islanders, age of puberty among,
Attractiveness of,
Offered as sacrifice to,
Small size of brain of,
Profounder sub-consciousness of,
Less hair on the body of,
Mental, moral and physical inferiority of,
Love of children of,
Greater length of life of,
Weaker muscles of,
Strength of affections of,
Vanity of,
Higher education of,
Shakespeare's opinion of,

Lord Birkenhead's opinion of,
Dean Inge's opinion of,
La Bruyère's opinion of,
Dr. Johnson's opinion of,
Mr. Oscar Browning's opinion of, . . .

Here I drew breath and added, indeed, in the margin, Why does Samuel Butler say, "Wise men never say what they think of women"? Wise men never say anything else apparently. But, I continued, leaning back in my chair and looking at the vast dome in which I was a single but by now somewhat harassed thought, what is so unfortunate is that wise men never think the same thing about women. Here is Pope:

Most women have no character at all.

And here is La Bruyère:

Les femmes sont extrêmes; elles sont meilleures ou
pires que les hommes—

a direct contradiction by keen observers who were contemporary. Are they capable of education or incapable? Napoleon thought them incapable. Dr. Johnson thought the opposite.[1] Have they souls or have they not souls? Some savages say they have none. Others, on the contrary, maintain that women are half divine and worship

[1] " 'Men know that women are an overmatch for them, and therefore they choose the weakest or the most ignorant. If they did not think so, they never could be afraid of women knowing as much as themselves.' . . . In justice to the sex, I think it but candid to acknowledge that, in a subsequent conversation, he told me that he was serious in what he said."—BOSWELL, *The Journal of a Tour to the Hebrides.*

them on that account.[1] Some sages hold that they are shallower in the brain; others that they are deeper in the consciousness. Goethe honoured them; Mussolini despises them. Wherever one looked men thought about women and thought differently. It was impossible to make head or tail of it all, I decided, glancing with envy at the reader next door who was making the neatest abstracts, headed often with an A or a B or a C, while my own notebook rioted with the wildest scribble of contradictory jottings. It was distressing, it was bewildering, it was humiliating. Truth had run through my fingers. Every drop had escaped.

I could not possibly go home, I reflected, and add as a serious contribution to the study of women and fiction that women have less hair on their bodies than men, or that the age of puberty among the South Sea Islanders is nine—or is it ninety?—even the handwriting had become in its distraction indecipherable. It was disgraceful to have nothing more weighty or respectable to show after a whole morning's work. And if I could not grasp the truth about W. (as for brevity's sake I had come to call her) in the past, why bother about W. in the future? It seemed pure waste of time to consult all those gentlemen who specialise in woman and her effect on whatever it may be—politics, children, wages, morality—numerous and learned as they are. One might as well leave their books unopened.

But while I pondered I had unconsciously, in my listlessness, in my desperation, been drawing a picture where I should, like my neighbour, have been writing a conclusion. I had been drawing a face, a figure. It was

1 "The ancient Germans believed that there was something holy in women, and accordingly consulted them as oracles."—FRAZER, The Golden Bough.

A ROOM OF ONE'S OWN

the face and the figure of Professor von X engaged in
writing his monumental work entitled *The Mental,
Moral, and Physical Inferiority of the Female Sex*. He
was not in my picture a man attractive to women. He
was heavily built; he had a great jowl; to balance that
he had very small eyes; he was very red in the face. His
expression suggested that he was labouring under some
emotion that made him jab his pen on the paper as if he
were killing some noxious insect as he wrote, but even
when he had killed it that did not satisfy him; he must
go on killing it; and even so, some cause for anger and
irritation remained. Could it be his wife, I asked, looking
at my picture. Was she in love with a cavalry officer?
Was the cavalry officer slim and elegant and dressed in
astrachan? Had he been laughed at, to adopt the Freudian
theory, in his cradle by a pretty girl? For even in his
cradle the professor, I thought, could not have been an
attractive child. Whatever the reason, the professor was
made to look very angry and very ugly in my sketch, as
he wrote his great book upon the mental, moral and
physical inferiority of women. Drawing pictures was an
idle way of finishing an unprofitable morning's work.
Yet it is in our idleness, in our dreams, that the sub-
merged truth sometimes comes to the top. A very elementary exercise in psychology, not to be dignified by
the name of psycho-analysis, showed me, on looking at
my notebook, that the sketch of the angry professor had
been made in anger. Anger had snatched my pencil while
I dreamt. But what was anger doing there? Interest,
confusion, amusement, boredom—all these emotions I
could trace and name as they succeeded each other
throughout the morning. Had anger, the black snake,
been lurking among them? Yes, said the sketch, anger

had. It referred me unmistakably to the one book, to the one phrase, which had roused the demon; it was the professor's statement about the mental, moral and physical inferiority of women. My heart had leapt. My cheeks had burnt. I had flushed with anger. There was nothing specially remarkable, however foolish, in that. One does not like to be told that one is naturally the inferior of a little man—I looked at the student next me—who breathes hard, wears a ready-made tie, and has not shaved this fortnight. One has certain foolish vanities. It is only human nature, I reflected, and began drawing cart-wheels and circles over the angry professor's face till he looked like a burning bush or a flaming comet—anyhow, an apparition without human semblance or significance. The professor was nothing now but a faggot burning on the top of Hampstead Heath. Soon my own anger was explained and done with; but curiosity remained. How explain the anger of the professors? Why were they angry? For when it came to analysing the impression left by these books there was always an element of heat. This heat took many forms; it showed itself in satire, in sentiment, in curiosity, in reprobation. But there was another element which was often present and could not immediately be identified. Anger, I called it. But it was anger that had gone underground and mixed itself with all kinds of other emotions. To judge from its odd effects, it was anger disguised and complex, not anger simple and open.

Whatever the reason, all these books, I thought, surveying the pile on the desk, are worthless for my purposes. They were worthless scientifically, that is to say, though humanly they were full of instruction, interest, boredom, and very queer facts about the habits of the

Fiji Islanders. They had been written in the red light of emotion and not in the white light of truth. Therefore they must be returned to the central desk and restored each to his own cell in the enormous honeycomb. All that I had retrieved from that morning's work had been the one fact of anger. The professors—I lumped them together thus—were angry. But why, I asked myself, having returned the books, why, I repeated, standing under the colonnade among the pigeons and the prehistoric canoes, why are they angry? And, asking myself this question, I strolled off to find a place for luncheon. What is the real nature of what I call for the moment their anger? I asked. Here was a puzzle that would last all the time that it takes to be served with food in a small restaurant somewhere near the British Museum. Some previous luncher had left the lunch edition of the evening paper on a chair, and, waiting to be served, I began idly reading the headlines. A ribbon of very large letters ran across the page. Somebody had made a big score in South Africa. Lesser ribbons announced that Sir Austen Chamberlain was at Geneva. A meat axe with human hair on it had been found in a cellar. Mr. Justice ____ commented in the Divorce Courts upon the Shamelessness of Women. Sprinkled about the paper were other pieces of news. A film actress had been lowered from a peak in California and hung suspended in mid-air. The weather was going to be foggy. The most transient visitor to this planet, I thought, who picked up this paper could not fail to be aware, even from this scattered testimony, that England is under the rule of a patriarchy. Nobody in their senses could fail to detect the dominance of the professor. His was the power and the money and the influence. He was the proprietor of the paper and its editor and sub-editor. He was the Foreign Secretary and the Judge. He was the cricketer; he owned the race-horses and the yachts. He was the director of the company that pays two hundred per cent to its shareholders. He left millions to charities and colleges that were ruled by himself. He suspended the film actress in mid-air. He will decide if the hair on the meat axe is human; he it is who will acquit or convict the murderer, and hang him, or let him go free. With the exception of the fog he seemed to control everything. Yet he was angry. I knew that he was angry by this token. When I read what he wrote about women I thought, not of what he was saying, but of himself. When an arguer argues dispassionately he thinks only of the argument; and the reader cannot help thinking of the argument too. If he had written dispassionately about women, had used indisputable proofs to establish his argument and had shown no trace of wishing that the result should be one thing rather than another, one would not have been angry either. One would have accepted the fact, as one accepts the fact that a pea is green or a canary yellow. So be it, I should have said. But I had been angry because he was angry. Yet it seemed absurd, I thought, turning over the evening paper, that a man with all this power should be angry. Or is anger, I wondered, somehow, the familiar, the attendant sprite on power? Rich people, for example, are often angry because they suspect that the poor want to seize their wealth. The professors, or patriarchs, as it might be more accurate to call them, might be angry for that reason partly, but partly for one that lies a little less obviously on the surface. Possibly they were not "angry" at all; often, indeed, they were admiring, devoted, exemplary in the relations of private life. Possibly when the professor insisted a little too emphatically upon the inferiority of women, he was concerned not with their inferiority, but with his own superiority. That was what he was protecting rather hot-headedly and with too much emphasis, because it was a jewel to him of the rarest price. Life for both sexes—and I looked at them, shouldering their way along the pavement—is arduous, difficult, a perpetual struggle. It calls for gigantic courage and strength. More than anything, perhaps, creatures of illusion as we are, it calls for confidence in oneself. Without self-confidence we are as babes in the cradle. And how can we generate this imponderable quality, which is yet so invaluable, most quickly? By thinking that other people are inferior to oneself. By feeling that one has some innate superiority—it may be wealth, or rank, a straight nose, or the portrait of a grandfather by Romney—for there is no end to the pathetic devices of the human imagination—over other people. Hence the enormous importance to a patriarch who has to conquer, who has to rule, of feeling that great numbers of people, half the human race indeed, are by nature inferior to himself. It must indeed be one of the chief sources of his power. But let me turn the light of this observation on to real life, I thought. Does it help to explain some of those psychological puzzles that one notes in the margin of daily life? Does it explain my astonishment the other day when Z, most humane, most modest of men, taking up some book by Rebecca West and reading a passage in it, exclaimed, "The arrant feminist! She says that men are snobs!" The exclamation, to me so surprising—for why was Miss West an arrant feminist for making a possibly true if uncomplimentary statement about the other sex?—was not merely the cry of wounded vanity; it was a protest against some infringement of his power to believe in himself. Women have served all these centuries as looking-glasses possessing the magic and delicious power of reflecting the figure of man at twice its natural size. Without that power probably the earth would still be swamp and jungle. The glories of all our wars would be unknown. We should still be scratching the outlines of deer on the remains of mutton bones and bartering flints for sheepskins or whatever simple ornament took our unsophisticated taste. Supermen and Fingers of Destiny would never have existed. The Czar and the Kaiser would never have worn their crowns or lost them. Whatever may be their use in civilised societies, mirrors are essential to all violent and heroic action. That is why Napoleon and Mussolini both insist so emphatically upon the inferiority of women, for if they were not inferior, they would cease to enlarge. That serves to explain in part the necessity that women so often are to men. And it serves to explain how restless they are under her criticism; how impossible it is for her to say to them this book is bad, this picture is feeble, or whatever it may be, without giving far more pain and rousing far more anger than a man would do who gave the same criticism. For if she begins to tell the truth, the figure in the looking-glass shrinks; his fitness for life is diminished. How is he to go on giving judgment, civilising natives, making laws, writing books, dressing up and speechifying at banquets, unless he can see himself at breakfast and at dinner at least twice the size he really is? So I reflected, crumbling my bread and stirring my coffee and now and again looking at the people in the street. The looking-glass vision is of supreme importance because it changes the vitality; it stimulates the nervous system. Take it away and man may die, like the drug fiend deprived of his cocaine. Under the spell of that illusion, I thought, looking out of the window, half the people on the pavement are striding to work. They put on their hats and coats in the morning under its agreeable rays. They start the day confident, braced, believing themselves desired at Miss Smith's tea party; they say to themselves as they go into the room, I am the superior of half the people here, and it is thus that they speak with that self-confidence, that self-assurance, which have had such profound consequences in public life and lead to such curious notes in the margin of the private mind.

But these contributions to the dangerous and fascinating subject of the psychology of the other sex—it is one, I hope, that you will investigate when you have five hundred a year of your own—were interrupted by the necessity of paying the bill. It came to five shillings and ninepence. I gave the waiter a ten-shilling note and he went to bring me change. There was another ten-shilling note in my purse; I noticed it, because it is a fact that still takes my breath away—the power of my purse to breed ten-shilling notes automatically. I open it and there they are. Society gives me chicken and coffee, bed and lodging, in return for a certain number of pieces of paper which were left me by an aunt, for no other reason than that I share her name.

My aunt, Mary Beton, I must tell you, died by a fall from her horse when she was riding out to take the air in Bombay. The news of my legacy reached me one night about the same time that the act was passed that gave votes to women. A solicitor's letter fell into the post-box and when I opened it I found that she had left me five hundred pounds a year for ever. Of the two—the vote and the money—the money, I own, seemed infinitely the more important. Before that I had made my living by cadging odd jobs from newspapers, by reporting a donkey show here or a wedding there; I had earned a few pounds by addressing envelopes, reading to old ladies, making artificial flowers, teaching the alphabet to small children in a kindergarten. Such were the chief occupations that were open to women before 1918. I need not, I am afraid, describe in any detail the hardness of the work, for you know perhaps women who have done it; nor the difficulty of living on the money when it was earned, for you may have tried. But what still remains with me as a worse infliction than either was the poison of fear and bitterness which those days bred in me. To begin with, always to be doing work that one did not wish to do, and to do it like a slave, flattering and fawning, not always necessarily perhaps, but it seemed necessary and the stakes were too great to run risks; and then the thought of that one gift which it was death to hide—a small one but dear to the possessor—perishing and with it myself, my soul—all this became like a rust eating away the bloom of the spring, destroying the tree at its heart. However, as I say, my aunt died; and whenever I change a ten-shilling note a little of that rust and corrosion is rubbed off; fear and bitterness go. Indeed, I thought, slipping the silver into my purse, it is remarkable, remembering the bitterness of those days, what a change of temper a fixed income will bring about. No force in the world can take from me my five hundred pounds. Food, house and clothing are mine for ever. Therefore not merely do effort and labour cease, but also hatred and bitterness.

I need not hate any man; he cannot hurt me. I need not flatter any man; he has nothing to give me. So imperceptibly I found myself adopting a new attitude towards the other half of the human race. It was absurd to blame any class or any sex, as a whole. Great bodies of people are never responsible for what they do. They are driven by instincts which are not within their control. They too, the patriarchs, the professors, had endless difficulties, terrible drawbacks to contend with. Their education had been in some ways as faulty as my own. It had bred in them defects as great. True, they had money and power, but only at the cost of harbouring in their breasts an eagle, a vulture, for ever tearing the liver out and plucking at the lungs—the instinct for possession, the rage for acquisition which drives them to desire other people's fields and goods perpetually; to make frontiers and flags; battleships and poison gas; to offer up their own lives and their children's lives. Walk through the Admiralty Arch (I had reached that monument), or any other avenue given up to trophies and cannon, and reflect upon the kind of glory celebrated there. Or watch in the spring sunshine the stockbroker and the great barrister going indoors to make money and more money and more money when it is a fact that five hundred pounds a year will keep one alive in the sunshine. These are unpleasant instincts to harbour, I reflected. They are bred of the conditions of life; of the lack of civilisation, I thought, looking at the statue of the Duke of Cambridge, and in particular at the feathers in his cocked hat, with a fixity that they have scarcely ever received before. And, as I realised these drawbacks, by degrees fear and bitterness modified themselves into pity and toleration; and then in a year or two, pity and toleration went, and the greatest release of all came, which is freedom to think of things in themselves. That building, for example, do I like it or not? Is that picture beautiful or not? Is that in my opinion a good book or a bad? Indeed my aunt's legacy unveiled the sky to me, and substituted for the large and imposing figure of a gentleman, which Milton recommended for my perpetual adoration, a view of the open sky.

So thinking, so speculating, I found my way back to my house by the river. Lamps were being lit and an indescribable change had come over London since the morning hour. It was as if the great machine after labouring all day had made with our help a few yards of something very exciting and beautiful—a fiery fabric flashing with red eyes, a tawny monster roaring with hot breath. Even the wind seemed flung like a flag as it lashed the houses and rattled the hoardings.

In my little street, however, domesticity prevailed. The house painter was descending his ladder; the nurse-maid was wheeling the perambulator carefully in and out back to nursery tea; the coal-heaver was folding his empty sacks on top of each other; the woman who keeps the green-grocer's shop was adding up the day's takings with her hands in red mittens. But so engrossed was I with the problem you have laid upon my shoulders that I could not see even these usual sights without referring them to one centre. I thought how much harder it is now than it must have been even a century ago to say which of these employments is the higher, the more necessary. Is it better to be a coal-heaver or a nursemaid; is the charwoman who has brought up eight children of less value to the world than the barrister who has made a hundred thousand pounds? It is useless to ask such questions; for nobody can answer them. Not only do the comparative values of charwomen and lawyers rise and fall from decade to decade, but we have no rods with which to measure them even as they are at the moment. I had been foolish to ask my professor to furnish me with "indisputable proofs" of this or that in his argument about women. Even if one could state the value of any one gift at the moment, those values will change; in a century's time very possibly they will have changed completely. Moreover, in a hundred years, I thought, reaching my own doorstep, women will have ceased to be the protected sex. Logically they will take part in all the activities and exertions that were once denied them. The nursemaid will heave coal. The shop-woman will drive an engine. All assumptions founded on the facts observed when women were the protected sex will have disappeared—as, for example (here a squad of soldiers marched down the street), that women and clergymen and gardeners live longer than other people. Remove that protection, expose them to the same exertions and activities, make them soldiers and sailors and engine-drivers and dock labourers, and will not women die off so much younger, so much quicker, than men that one will say, "I saw a woman today," as one used to say, "I saw an aeroplane"? Anything may happen when womanhood has ceased to be a protected occupation, I thought, opening the door. But what bearing has all this upon the subject of my paper, Women and Fiction? I asked, going indoors.

THREE

It was disappointing not to have brought back in the evening some important statement, some authentic fact. Women are poorer than men because—this or that. Perhaps now it would be better to give up seeking for the truth, and receiving on one's head an avalanche of opinion hot as lava, discoloured as dish-water. It would be better to draw the curtains; to shut out distractions; to light the lamp; to narrow the enquiry and to ask the historian, who records not opinions but facts, to describe under what conditions women lived, not throughout the ages, but in England, say in the time of Elizabeth.

For it is a perennial puzzle why no woman wrote a word of that extraordinary literature when every other man, it seemed, was capable of song or sonnet. What were the conditions in which women lived, I asked myself; for fiction, imaginative work that is, is not dropped like a pebble upon the ground, as science may be; fiction is like a spider's web, attached ever so lightly perhaps, but still attached to life at all four corners. Often the attachment is scarcely perceptible; Shakespeare's plays, for instance, seem to hang there complete by themselves. But when the web is pulled askew, hooked up at the edge, torn in the middle, one remembers that these webs are not spun in mid-air by incorporeal creatures, but are the work of suffering human beings, and are attached to grossly material things, like health and money and the houses we live in.

I went, therefore, to the shelf where the histories stand and took down one of the latest, Professor Trevelyan's *History of England*. Once more I looked up Women, found "position of," and turned to the pages indicated. "Wife-beating," I read, "was a recognised right of man, and was practised without shame by high as well as low. . . . Similarly," the historian goes on, "the daughter who refused to marry the gentleman of her parents' choice was liable to be locked up, beaten and flung about the room, without any shock being inflicted on public opinion. Marriage was not an affair of personal affection, but of family avarice, particularly in the 'chivalrous' upper classes. . . . Betrothal often took place while one or both of the parties was in the cradle, and marriage when they were scarcely out of the nurses' charge." That was about 1470, soon after Chaucer's time. The next reference to the position of women is some two hundred years later, in the time of the Stuarts. "It was still the exception for women of the upper and middle class to choose their own husbands, and when the husband had been assigned, he was lord and master, so far at least as law and custom could make him. Yet even so," Professor Trevelyan concludes, "neither Shakespeare's women nor those of authentic seventeenth-century memoirs, like the Verneys and the Hutchinsons, seem wanting in personality and character." Certainly, if we consider it, Cleopatra must have had a way with her; Lady Macbeth, one would suppose, had a will of her own; Rosalind, one might conclude, was an attractive girl. Professor Trevelyan is speaking no more than the truth when he remarks that Shakespeare's women do not seem wanting in personality and character. Not being a historian, one might go even further and say that women have burnt like beacons in all the works of all the poets from the beginning of time—Clytemnestra, Antigone, Cleopatra, Lady Macbeth, Phèdre, Cressida, Rosalind, Desdemona, the Duchess of Malfi, among the dramatists; then among the prose writers: Millamant, Clarissa, Becky Sharp, Anna Karenina, Emma Bovary, Madame de Guermantes—the names flock to mind, nor do they recall women "lacking in personality and character." Indeed, if woman had no existence save in the fiction written by men, one would imagine her a person of the utmost importance; very various; heroic and mean; splendid and sordid; infinitely beautiful and hideous in the extreme; as great as a man, some think even greater.[1]

1 "It remains a strange and almost inexplicable fact that in Athena's city, where women were kept in almost Oriental suppression as odalisques or drudges, the stage should yet have produced figures like Clytemnestra and Cassandra, Atossa and Antigone, Phèdre and Medea, and all the other heroines who dominate play after play of the 'misogynist' Euripides. But the paradox of this world where in real life a respectable woman could hardly show her face alone in the street, and yet on the stage woman equals or surpasses man, has never been satisfactorily explained. In modern tragedy the same predominance exists. At all events, a very cursory survey of Shakespeare's work (similarly with Webster, though not with Marlowe or Jonson)

But this is woman in fiction. In fact, as Professor Trevelyan points out, she was locked up, beaten and flung about the room.

A very queer, composite being thus emerges. Imaginatively she is of the highest importance; practically she is completely insignificant. She pervades poetry from cover to cover; she is all but absent from history. She dominates the lives of kings and conquerors in fiction; in fact she was the slave of any boy whose parents forced a ring upon her finger. Some of the most inspired words, some of the most profound thoughts in literature fall from her lips; in real life she could hardly read, could scarcely spell, and was the property of her husband.

It was certainly an odd monster that one made up by reading the historians first and the poets afterwards—a worm winged like an eagle; the spirit of life and beauty in a kitchen chopping up suet. But these monsters, however amusing to the imagination, have no existence in fact. What one must do to bring her to life was to think poetically and prosaically at one and the same moment, thus keeping in touch with fact—that she is Mrs. Martin, aged thirty-six, dressed in blue, wearing a black hat and brown shoes; but not losing sight of fiction either—that she is a vessel in which all sorts of spirits and forces are coursing and flashing perpetually. The moment, however, that one tries this method with the Elizabethan woman, one branch of illumination fails; one is held up by the scarcity of facts. One knows nothing detailed,

suffices to reveal how this dominance, this initiative of women, persists from Rosalind to Lady Macbeth. So too in Racine; six of his tragedies bear their heroines' names; and what male characters of his shall we set against Hermione and Andromaque, Bérénice and Roxane, Phèdre and Athalie? So again with Ibsen; what men shall we match with Solveig and Nora, Hedda and Hilda Wangel and Rebecca West?"—F. L. LUCAS, Tragedy, pp. 114–15.

nothing perfectly true and substantial about her. History scarcely mentions her. And I turned to Professor Trevelyan again to see what history meant to him. I found by looking at his chapter headings that it meant—

"The Manor Court and the Methods of Open-field Agriculture . . . The Cistercians and Sheep-farming . . . The Crusades . . . The University . . . The House of Commons . . . The Hundreds Years' War . . . The Wars of the Roses . . . The Renaissance Scholars . . . The Dissolution of the Monasteries . . . Agrarian and Religious Strife . . . The Origin of English Sea-power . . . The Armada . . ." and so on. Occasionally an individual woman is mentioned, an Elizabeth, or a Mary; a queen or a great lady. But by no possible means could middle-class women with nothing but brains and character at their command have taken part in any one of the great movements which, brought together, constitute the historian's view of the past. Nor shall we find her in any collection of anecdotes. Aubrey hardly mentions her. She never writes her own life and scarcely keeps a diary; there are only a handful of her letters in existence. She left no plays or poems by which we can judge her. What one wants, I thought—and why does not some brilliant student at Newnham or Girton supply it?—is a mass of information; at what age did she marry; how many children had she as a rule; what was her house like; had she a room to herself; did she do the cooking; would she be likely to have a servant? All these facts lie somewhere, presumably, in parish registers and account books; the life of the average Elizabethan woman must be scattered about somewhere, could one collect it and make a book of it. It would be ambitious beyond my daring, I thought, looking about the shelves for books that were not there, to suggest to the students of those famous colleges that they should re-write history, though I own that it often seems a little queer as it is, unreal, lop-sided; but why should they not add a supplement to history? calling it, of course, by some inconspicuous name so that women might figure there without impropriety? For one often catches a glimpse of them in the lives of the great, whisking away into the background, concealing, I sometimes think, a wink, a laugh, perhaps a tear. And, after all, we have lives enough of Jane Austen; it scarcely seems necessary to consider again the influence of the tragedies of Joanna Baillie upon the poetry of Edgar Allan Poe; as for myself, I should not mind if the homes and haunts of Mary Russell Mitford were closed to the public for a century at least. But what I find deplorable, I continued, looking about the bookshelves again, is that nothing is known about women before the eighteenth century. I have no model in my mind to turn about this way and that. Here am I asking why women did not write poetry in the Elizabethan age, and I am not sure how they were educated; whether they were taught to write; whether they had sitting-rooms to themselves; how many women had children before they were twenty-one; what, in short, they did from eight in the morning till eight at night. They had no money evidently; according to Professor Trevelyan they were married whether they liked it or not before they were out of the nursery, at fifteen or sixteen very likely. It would have been extremely odd, even upon this showing, had one of them suddenly written the plays of Shakespeare, I concluded, and I thought of that old gentleman, who is dead now, but was a bishop, I think, who declared that it was impossible for any woman, past, present, or to come, to have the genius of Shakespeare. He wrote to the papers about it. He also told a lady who applied to him for information that cats do not as a matter of fact go to heaven, though they have, he added, souls of a sort. How much thinking those old gentlemen used to save one! How the borders of ignorance shrank back at their approach! Cats do not go to heaven. Women cannot write the plays of Shakespeare.

Be that as it may, I could not help thinking, as I looked at the works of Shakespeare on the shelf, that the bishop was right at least in this; it would have been impossible, completely and entirely, for any woman to have written the plays of Shakespeare in the age of Shakespeare. Let me imagine, since facts are so hard to come by, what would have happened had Shakespeare had a wonderfully gifted sister, called Judith, let us say. Shakespeare himself went, very probably—his mother was an heiress—to the grammar school, where he may have learnt Latin—Ovid, Virgil and Horace—and the elements of grammar and logic. He was, it is well known, a wild boy who poached rabbits, perhaps shot a deer, and had, rather sooner than he should have done, to marry a woman in the neighbourhood, who bore him a child rather quicker than was right. That escapade sent him to seek his fortune in London. He had, it seemed, a taste for the theatre; he began by holding horses at the stage door. Very soon he got work in the theatre, became a successful actor, and lived at the hub of the universe, meeting everybody, knowing everybody, practising his art on the boards, exercising his wits in the streets, and even getting access to the palace of the queen. Meanwhile his extraordinarily gifted sister, let us suppose, remained at home. She was as adventurous, as imaginative, as agog to see the world as he was. But she was not sent to school. She had no chance of learning grammar and logic, let alone of reading Horace and Virgil. She picked up a book now and then, one of her brother's perhaps, and read a few pages. But then her parents came in and told her to mend the stockings or mind the stew and not moon about with books and papers. They would have spoken sharply but kindly, for they were substantial people who knew the conditions of life for a woman and loved their daughter—indeed, more likely than not she was the apple of her father's eye. Perhaps she scribbled some pages up in an apple loft on the sly, but was careful to hide them or set fire to them. Soon, however, before she was out of her teens, she was to be betrothed to the son of a neighbouring wool-stapler. She cried out that marriage was hateful to her, and for that she was severely beaten by her father. Then he ceased to scold her. He begged her instead not to hurt him, not to shame him in this matter of her marriage. He would give her a chain of beads or a fine petticoat, he said; and there were tears in his eyes. How could she disobey him? How could she break his heart? The force of her own gift alone drove her to it. She made up a small parcel of her belongings, let herself down by a rope one summer's night and took the road to London. She was not seventeen. The birds that sang in the hedge were not more musical than she was. She had the quickest fancy, a gift like her brother's, for the tune of words. Like him, she had a taste for the theatre. She stood at the stage door; she wanted to act, she said. Men laughed in her face. The manager—a fat, loose-lipped man—guffawed. He bellowed something about poodles dancing and women acting—no woman, he said, could possibly be an actress.

He hinted—you can imagine what. She could get no training in her craft. Could she even seek her dinner in a tavern or roam the streets at midnight? Yet her genius was for fiction and lusted to feed abundantly upon the lives of men and women and the study of their ways. At last—for she was very young, oddly like Shakespeare the poet in her face, with the same grey eyes and rounded brows—at last Nick Greene the actor-manager took pity on her; she found herself with child by that gentleman and so—who shall measure the heat and violence of the poet's heart when caught and tangled in a woman's body?—killed herself one winter's night and lies buried at some cross-roads where the omnibuses now stop outside the Elephant and Castle.

That, more or less, is how the story would run, I think, if a woman in Shakespeare's day had had Shakespeare's genius. But for my part, I agree with the deceased bishop, if such he was—it is unthinkable that any woman in Shakespeare's day should have had Shakespeare's genius. For genius like Shakespeare's is not born among labouring, uneducated, servile people. It was not born in England among the Saxons and the Britons. It is not born today among the working classes. How, then, could it have been born among women whose work began, according to Professor Trevelyan, almost before they were out of the nursery, who were forced to it by their parents and held to it by all the power of law and custom? Yet genius of a sort must have existed among women as it must have existed among the working classes. Now and again an Emily Brontë or a Robert Burns blazes out and proves its presence. But certainly it never got itself on to paper. When, however, one reads of a witch being ducked, of a woman possessed by devils, of a wise woman selling herbs, or even of a very remarkable man who had a mother, then I think we are on the track of a lost novelist, a suppressed poet, of some mute and inglorious Jane Austen, some Emily Brontë who dashed her brains out on the moor or mopped and mowed about the highways crazed with the torture that her gift had put her to. Indeed, I would venture to guess that Anon, who wrote so many poems without signing them, was often a woman. It was a woman Edward Fitzgerald, I think, suggested who made the ballads and the folk-songs, crooning them to her children, beguiling her spinning with them, or the length of the winter's night.

This may be true or it may be false—who can say?—but what is true in it, so it seemed to me, reviewing the story of Shakespeare's sister as I had made it, is that any woman born with a great gift in the sixteenth century would certainly have gone crazed, shot herself, or ended her days in some lonely cottage outside the village, half witch, half wizard, feared and mocked at. For it needs little skill in psychology to be sure that a highly gifted girl who had tried to use her gift for poetry would have been so thwarted and hindered by other people, so tortured and pulled asunder by her own contrary instincts, that she must have lost her health and sanity to a certainty. No girl could have walked to London and stood at a stage door and forced her way into the presence of actor-managers without doing herself a violence and suffering an anguish which may have been irrational—for chastity may be a fetish invented by certain societies for unknown reasons—but were none the less inevitable. Chastity had then, it has even now, a religious importance in a woman's life, and has so wrapped itself round with nerves and instincts that to cut it free and bring it to the light of day demands courage of the rarest. To have lived a free life in London in the sixteenth century would have meant for a woman who was poet and playwright a nervous stress and dilemma which might well have killed her. Had she survived, whatever she had written would have been twisted and deformed, issuing from a strained and morbid imagination. And undoubtedly, I thought, looking at the shelf where there are no plays by women, her work would have gone unsigned. That refuge she would have sought certainly. It was the relic of the sense of chastity that dictated anonymity to women even so late as the nineteenth century. Currer Bell, George Eliot, George Sand, all the victims of inner strife as their writings prove, sought ineffectively to veil themselves by using the name of a man. Thus they did homage to the convention, which if not implanted by the other sex was liberally encouraged by them (the chief glory of a woman is not to be talked of, said Pericles, himself a much-talked-of man), that publicity in women is detestable. Anonymity runs in their blood. The desire to be veiled still possesses them. They are not even now as concerned about the health of their fame as men are, and, speaking generally, will pass a tombstone or a signpost without feeling an irresistible desire to cut their names on it, as Alf, Bert or Chas. must do in obedience to their instinct, which murmurs if it sees a fine woman go by, or even a dog, Ce chien est à moi. And, of course, it may not be a dog, I thought, remembering Parliament Square, the Sièges Allée and other avenues; it may be a piece of land or a man with curly black hair. It is one of the great advantages of being a woman that one can pass even a very fine negress without wishing to make an Englishwoman of her.

That woman, then, who was born with a gift of poetry in the sixteenth century, was an unhappy woman, a woman at strife against herself. All the conditions of her life, all her own instincts, were hostile to the state of mind which is needed to set free whatever is in the brain. But what is the state of mind that is most propitious to the act of creation, I asked. Can one come by any notion of the state that furthers and makes possible that strange activity? Here I opened the volume containing the Tragedies of Shakespeare. What was Shakespeare's state of mind, for instance, when he wrote *Lear* and *Antony and Cleopatra?* It was certainly the state of mind most favourable to poetry that there has ever existed. But Shakespeare himself said nothing about it. We only know casually and by chance that he "never blotted a line." Nothing indeed was ever said by the artist himself about his state of mind until the eighteenth century perhaps. Rousseau perhaps began it. At any rate, by the nineteenth century self-consciousness had developed so far that it was the habit for men of letters to describe their minds in confessions and autobiographies. Their lives also were written, and their letters were printed after their deaths. Thus, though we do not know what Shakespeare went through when he wrote *Lear*, we do know what Carlyle went through when he wrote the *French Revolution;* what Flaubert went through when he wrote *Madame Bovary;* what Keats was going through when he tried to write poetry against the coming of death and the indifference of the world.

And one gathers from this enormous modern literature

of confession and self-analysis that to write a work of genius is almost always a feat of prodigious difficulty. Everything is against the likelihood that it will come from the writer's mind whole and entire. Generally material circumstances are against it. Dogs will bark; people will interrupt; money must be made; health will break down. Further, accentuating all these difficulties and making them harder to bear is the world's notorious indifference. It does not ask people to write poems and novels and histories; it does not need them. It does not care whether Flaubert finds the right word or whether Carlyle scrupulously verifies this or that fact. Naturally, it will not pay for what it does not want. And so the writer, Keats, Flaubert, Carlyle, suffers, especially in the creative years of youth, every form of distraction and discouragement. A curse, a cry of agony, rises from those books of analysis and confession. "Mighty poets in their misery dead"—that is the burden of their song. If anything comes through in spite of all this, it is a miracle, and probably no book is born entire and uncrippled as it was conceived.

But for women, I thought, looking at the empty shelves, these difficulties were infinitely more formidable. In the first place, to have a room of her own, let alone a quiet room or a sound-proof room, was out of the question, unless her parents were exceptionally rich or very noble, even up to the beginning of the nineteenth century. Since her pin money, which depended on the good will of her father, was only enough to keep her clothed, she was debarred from such alleviations as came even to Keats or Tennyson or Carlyle, all poor men, from a walking tour, a little journey to France, from the separate lodging which, even if it were miserable enough, sheltered them from the claims and tyrannies of their families. Such material difficulties were formidable; but much worse were the immaterial. The indifference of the world which Keats and Flaubert and other men of genius have found so hard to bear was in her case not indifference but hostility. The world did not say to her as it said to them, Write if you choose; it makes no difference to me. The world said with a guffaw, Write? What's the good of your writing? Here the psychologists of Newnham and Girton might come to our help, I thought, looking again at the blank spaces on the shelves. For surely it is time that the effect of discouragement upon the mind of the artist should be measured, as I have seen a dairy company measure the effect of ordinary milk and Grade A milk upon the body of the rat. They set two rats in cages side by side, and of the two one was furtive, timid and small, and the other was glossy, bold and big. Now what food do we feed women as artists upon? I asked, remembering, I suppose, that dinner of prunes and custard. To answer that question I had only to open the evening paper and to read that Lord Birkenhead is of opinion—but really I am not going to trouble to copy out Lord Birkenhead's opinion upon the writing of women. What Dean Inge says I will leave in peace. The Harley Street specialist may be allowed to rouse the echoes of Harley Street with his vociferations without raising a hair on my head. I will quote, however, Mr. Oscar Browning, because Mr. Oscar Browning was a great figure in Cambridge at one time, and used to examine the students at Girton and Newnham. Mr. Oscar Browning was wont to declare "that the impression left on his mind, after looking over any set of examination papers, was that, irrespective of the marks he might give, the best woman was intellectually the inferior of the worst man." After saying that Mr. Browning went back to his rooms—and it is this sequel that endears him and makes him a human figure of some bulk and majesty— he went back to his rooms and found a stable-boy lying on the sofa—"a mere skeleton, his cheeks were cavernous and sallow, his teeth were black, and he did not appear to have the full use of his limbs. . . . 'That's Arthur' [said Mr. Browning]. 'He's a dear boy really and most high-minded.' " The two pictures always seem to me to complete each other. And happily in this age of biography the two pictures often do complete each other, so that we are able to interpret the opinions of great men not only by what they say, but by what they do.

But though this is possible now, such opinions coming from the lips of important people must have been formidable enough even fifty years ago. Let us suppose that a father from the highest motives did not wish his daughter to leave home and become writer, painter or scholar. "See what Mr. Oscar Browning says," he would say; and there was not only Mr. Oscar Browning; there was the *Saturday Review;* there was Mr. Greg—the "essentials of a woman's being," said Mr. Greg emphatically, "are that *they are supported by, and they minister to, men*"—there was an enormous body of masculine opinion to the effect that nothing could be expected of women intellectually. Even if her father did not read out loud these opinions, any girl could read them for herself; and the reading, even in the nineteenth century, must have lowered her vitality, and told profoundly upon her work. There would always have been that assertion— you cannot do this, you are incapable of doing that— to protest against, to overcome. Probably for a novelist this germ is no longer of much effect; for there have been women novelists of merit. But for painters it must still have some sting in it; and for musicians, I imagine, is even now active and poisonous in the extreme. The woman composer stands where the actress stood in the time of Shakespeare. Nick Greene, I thought, remembering the story I had made about Shakespeare's sister, said that a woman acting put him in mind of a dog dancing. Johnson repeated the phrase two hundred years later of women preaching. And here, I said, opening a book about music, we have the very words used again in this year of grace, 1928, of women who try to write music. "Of Mlle. Germaine Tailleferre one can only repeat Dr. Johnson's dictum concerning a woman preacher, transposed into terms of music. 'Sir, a woman's composing is like a dog's walking on his hind legs. It is not done well, but you are surprised to find it done at all.' "[1] So accurately does history repeat itself.

Thus, I concluded, shutting Mr. Oscar Browning's life and pushing away the rest, it is fairly evident that even in the nineteenth century a woman was not encouraged to be an artist. On the contrary, she was snubbed, slapped, lectured and exhorted. Her mind must have been strained and her vitality lowered by the need of opposing this, of disproving that. For here again we come within range of that very interesting and obscure masculine complex which has had so much influence upon the woman's movement; that deep-seated desire, not so much that *she* shall be inferior as that *he* shall be superior, which plants him wherever one looks, not only in front of the arts, but barring the way to politics too, even when the risk to himself seems infinitesimal and

[1] *A Survey of Contemporary Music*, Cecil Gray, p. 246.

the suppliant humble and devoted. Even Lady Bessborough, I remembered, with all her passion for politics,
must humbly bow herself and write to Lord Granville
Leveson-Gower: ". . . notwithstanding all my violence
in politics and talking so much on that subject, I perfectly
agree with you that no woman has any business to
meddle with that or any other serious business, farther
than giving her opinion (if she is ask'd)." And so she
goes on to spend her enthusiasm where it meets with no
obstacle whatsoever upon that immensely important
subject, Lord Granville's maiden speech in the House
of Commons. The spectacle is certainly a strange one, I
thought. The history of men's opposition to women's
emancipation is more interesting perhaps than the story
of that emancipation itself. An amusing book might be
made of it if some young student at Girton or Newnham
would collect examples and deduce a theory—but she
would need thick gloves on her hands, and bars to pro-
tect her of solid gold.

But what is amusing now, I recollected, shutting Lady
Bessborough, had to be taken in desperate earnest once.
Opinions that one now pastes in a book labelled cock-
a-doodle-dum and keeps for reading to select audiences
on summer nights once drew tears, I can assure you.
Among your grandmothers and great-grandmothers
there were many that wept their eyes out. Florence
Nightingale shrieked aloud in her agony.[1] Moreover, it
is all very well for you, who have got yourselves to
college and enjoy sitting-rooms—or is it only bed-sitting-
rooms?—of your own to say that genius should disregard such opinions; that genius should be above caring

[1] See *Cassandra*, by Florence Nightingale, printed in *The Cause*, by R.
Strachey.

what is said of it. Unfortunately, it is precisely the men or women of genius who mind most what is said of them. Remember Keats. Remember the words he had cut on his tombstone. Think of Tennyson; think—but I need hardly multiply instances of the undeniable, if very unfortunate, fact that it is the nature of the artist to mind excessively what is said about him. Literature is strewn with the wreckage of men who have minded beyond reason the opinions of others.

And this susceptibility of theirs is doubly unfortunate, I thought, returning again to my original enquiry into what state of mind is most propitious for creative work, because the mind of an artist, in order to achieve the prodigious effort of freeing whole and entire the work that is in him, must be incandescent, like Shakespeare's mind, I conjectured, looking at the book which lay open at *Antony and Cleopatra*. There must be no obstacle in it, no foreign matter unconsumed.

For though we say that we know nothing about Shakespeare's state of mind, even as we say that, we are saying something about Shakespeare's state of mind. The reason perhaps why we know so little of Shakespeare—compared with Donne or Ben Jonson or Milton—is that his grudges and spites and antipathies are hidden from us. We are not held up by some "revelation" which reminds us of the writer. All desire to protest, to preach, to proclaim an injury, to pay off a score, to make the world the witness of some hardship or grievance was fired out of him and consumed. Therefore his poetry flows from him free and unimpeded. If ever a human being got his work expressed completely, it was Shakespeare. If ever a mind was incandescent, unimpeded, I thought, turning again to the bookcase, it was Shakespeare's mind.

FOUR

That one would find any woman in that state of mind in the sixteenth century was obviously impossible. One has only to think of the Elizabethan tombstones with all those children kneeling with clasped hands; and their early deaths; and to see their houses with their dark, cramped rooms, to realise that no woman could have written poetry then. What one would expect to find would be that rather later perhaps some great lady would take advantage of her comparative freedom and comfort to publish something with her name to it and risk being thought a monster. Men, of course, are not snobs, I continued, carefully eschewing "the arrant feminism" of Miss Rebecca West; but they appreciate with sympathy for the most part the efforts of a countess to write verse. One would expect to find a lady of title meeting with far greater encouragement than an unknown Miss Austen or a Miss Brontë at that time would have met with. But one would also expect to find that her mind was disturbed by alien emotions like fear and hatred and that her poems showed traces of that disturbance. Here is Lady Winchilsea, for example, I thought, taking down her poems. She was born in the year 1661; she was noble both by birth and by marriage; she was childless; she wrote poetry, and one has only to open her poetry to find her bursting out in indignation against the position of women:

How are we fallen! fallen by mistaken rules,
And Education's more than Nature's fools;
Debarred from all improvements of the mind,
And to be dull, expected and designed;
And if some one would soar above the rest,
With warmer fancy, and ambition pressed,
So strong the opposing faction still appears,
The hopes to thrive can ne'er outweigh the fears.

Clearly her mind has by no means "consumed all impediments and become incandescent." On the contrary, it is harassed and distracted with hates and grievances. The human race is split up for her into two parties. Men are the "opposing faction"; men are hated and feared, because they have the power to bar her way to what she wants to do—which is to write.

Alas! a woman that attempts the pen,
Such a presumptuous creature is esteemed,
The fault can by no virtue be redeemed.
They tell us we mistake our sex and way;
Good breeding, fashion, dancing, dressing, play,
Are the accomplishments we should desire;

To write, or read, or think, or to enquire,
Would cloud our beauty, and exhaust our time,
And interrupt the conquests of our prime,
Whilst the dull manage of a servile house
Is held by some our utmost art and use.

Indeed she has to encourage herself to write by supposing that what she writes will never be published; to soothe herself with the sad chant:

To some few friends, and to thy sorrows sing,
For groves of laurel thou wert never meant;
Be dark enough thy shades, and be thou there content.

Yet it is clear that could she have freed her mind from hate and fear and not heaped it with bitterness and resentment, the fire was hot within her. Now and again words issue of pure poetry:

Nor will in fading silks compose,
Faintly the inimitable rose.

—they are rightly praised by Mr. Murry, and Pope, it is thought, remembered and appropriated those others:

Now the jonquille o'ercomes the feeble brain;
We faint beneath the aromatic pain.

It was a thousand pities that the woman who could write like that, whose mind was turned to nature and reflection, should have been forced to anger and bitterness. But how could she have helped herself? I asked, imagining the sneers and the laughter, the adulation of the

64

toadies, the scepticism of the professional poet. She must have shut herself up in a room in the country to write, and been torn asunder by bitterness and scruples perhaps, though her husband was of the kindest, and their married life perfection. She "must have," I say, because when one comes to seek out the facts about Lady Winchilsea, one finds, as usual, that almost nothing is known about her. She suffered terribly from melancholy, which we can explain at least to some extent when we find her telling us how in the grip of it she would imagine:

> *My lines decried, and my employment thought,*
> *An useless folly or presumptuous fault:*

The employment, which was thus censured, was, as far as one can see, the harmless one of rambling about the fields and dreaming:

> *My hand delights to trace unusual things,*
> *And deviates from the known and common way,*
> *Nor will in fading silks compose,*
> *Faintly the inimitable rose.*

Naturally, if that was her habit and that was her delight, she could only expect to be laughed at; and, accordingly, Pope or Gay is said to have satirised her "as a bluestocking with an itch for scribbling." Also it is thought that she offended Gay by laughing at him. She said that his *Trivia* showed that "he was more proper to walk before a chair than to ride in one." But this is all "dubious gossip" and, says Mr. Murry, "uninteresting." But there I do not agree with him, for I should have liked to have had more even of dubious gossip so that I might have found out or made up some image of this melancholy lady, who loved wandering in the fields and thinking about unusual things and scorned, so rashly, so unwisely, "the dull manage of a servile house." But she became diffuse, Mr. Murry says. Her gift is all grown about with weeds and bound with briars. It had no chance of showing itself for the fine distinguished gift it was. And so, putting her back on the shelf, I turned to the other great lady, the Duchess whom Lamb loved, hare-brained, fantastical Margaret of Newcastle, her elder, but her contemporary. They were very different, but alike in this that both were noble and both childless, and both were married to the best of husbands. In both burnt the same passion for poetry and both are disfigured and deformed by the same causes. Open the Duchess and one finds the same outburst of rage, "Women live like Bats or Owls, labour like Beasts, and die like Worms. . . ." Margaret too might have been a poet; in our day all that activity would have turned a wheel of some sort. As it was, what could bind, tame or civilise for human use that wild, generous, untutored intelligence? It poured itself out, higgledy-piggledy, in torrents of rhyme and prose, poetry and philosophy which stand congealed in quartos and folios that nobody ever reads. She should have had a microscope put in her hand. She should have been taught to look at the stars and reason scientifically. Her wits were turned with solitude and freedom. No one checked her. No one taught her. The professors fawned on her. At Court they jeered at her. Sir Egerton Brydges complained of her coarseness—"as flowing from a female of high rank brought up in the Courts." She shut herself up at Welbeck alone.

What a vision of loneliness and riot the thought of

Margaret Cavendish brings to mind! as if some giant cucumber had spread itself over all the roses and carnations in the garden and choked them to death. What a waste that the woman who wrote "the best bred women are those whose minds are civilest" should have frittered her time away scribbling nonsense and plunging ever deeper into obscurity and folly till the people crowded round her coach when she issued out. Evidently the crazy Duchess became a bogey to frighten clever girls with. Here, I remembered, putting away the Duchess and opening Dorothy Osborne's letters, is Dorothy writing to Temple about the Duchess's new book. "Sure the poore woman is a little distracted, shee could never bee soe rediculous else as to venture at writeing book's and in verse too, if I should not sleep this fortnight I should not come to that."

And so, since no woman of sense and modesty could write books, Dorothy, who was sensitive and melancholy, the very opposite of the Duchess in temper, wrote nothing. Letters did not count. A woman might write letters while she was sitting by her father's sick-bed. She could write them by the fire whilst the men talked without disturbing them. The strange thing is, I thought, turning over the pages of Dorothy's letters, what a gift that untaught and solitary girl had for the framing of a sentence, for the fashioning of a scene. Listen to her running on:

"After dinner wee sitt and talk till Mr. B. com's in question and then I am gon. the heat of the day is spent in reading or working and about sixe or seven a Clock, I walke out into a Common that lyes hard by the house where a great many young wenches keep Sheep and Cow's and sitt in the shades singing of Ballads; I goe to

them and compare their voyces and Beauty's to some
Ancient Shepherdesses that I have read of and finde a
vaste difference there, but trust mee I think these are as
innocent as those could bee. I talke to them, and finde
they want nothing to make them the happiest People in
the world, but the knoledge that they are soe. most
commonly when we are in the middest of our discourse
one looks about her and spyes her Cow's goeing into
the Corne and then away they all run, as if they had
wing's at theire heels. I that am not soe nimble stay
behinde, and when I see them driveing home theire Cattle I think tis time for mee to retyre too. when I have
supped I goe into the Garden and soe to the syde of a
small River that runs by it where I sitt downe and wish
you with mee. . . ."

One could have sworn that she had the makings of a
writer in her. But "if I should not sleep this fortnight I
should not come to that"—one can measure the opposition that was in the air to a woman writing when one
finds that even a woman with a great turn for writing
has brought herself to believe that to write a book was
to be ridiculous, even to show oneself distracted. And
so we come, I continued, replacing the single short volume of Dorothy Osborne's letters upon the shelf, to
Mrs. Behn.

And with Mrs. Behn we turn a very important corner
on the road. We leave behind, shut up in their parks
among their folios, those solitary great ladies who wrote
without audience or criticism, for their own delight
alone. We come to town and rub shoulders with ordinary
people in the streets. Mrs. Behn was a middle-class
woman with all the plebeian virtues of humour, vitality
and courage; a woman forced by the death of her hus-

band and some unfortunate adventures of her own to make her living by her wits. She had to work on equal terms with men. She made, by working very hard, enough to live on. The importance of that fact outweighs anything that she actually wrote, even the splendid "A Thousand Martyrs I have made," or "Love in Fantastic Triumph sat," for here begins the freedom of the mind, or rather the possibility that in the course of time the mind will be free to write what it likes. For now that Aphra Behn had done it, girls could go to their parents and say, You need not give me an allowance; I can make money by my pen. Of course the answer for many years to come was, Yes, by living the life of Aphra Behn! Death would be better! and the door was slammed faster than ever. That profoundly interesting subject, the value that men set upon women's chastity and its effect upon their education, here suggests itself for discussion, and might provide an interesting book if any student at Girton or Newnham cared to go into the matter. Lady Dudley, sitting in diamonds among the midges of a Scottish moor, might serve for frontispiece. Lord Dudley, *The Times* said when Lady Dudley died the other day, "a man of cultivated taste and many accomplishments, was benevolent and bountiful, but whimsically despotic. He insisted upon his wife's wearing full dress, even at the remotest shooting-lodge in the Highlands; he loaded her with gorgeous jewels," and so on, "he gave her everything—always excepting any measure of responsibility." Then Lord Dudley had a stroke and she nursed him and ruled his estates with supreme competence for ever after. That whimsical despotism was in the nineteenth century too.

But to return. Aphra Behn proved that money could

be made by writing at the sacrifice, perhaps, of certain agreeable qualities; and so by degrees writing became not merely a sign of folly and a distracted mind, but was of practical importance. A husband might die, or some disaster overtake the family. Hundreds of women began as the eighteenth century drew on to add to their pin money, or to come to the rescue of their families by making translations or writing the innumerable bad novels which have ceased to be recorded even in text-books, but are to be picked up in the fourpenny boxes in the Charing Cross Road. The extreme activity of mind which showed itself in the later eighteenth century among women—the talking, and the meeting, the writing of essays on Shakespeare, the translating of the classics—was founded on the solid fact that women could make money by writing. Money dignifies what is frivolous if unpaid for. It might still be well to sneer at "blue-stockings with an itch for scribbling," but it could not be denied that they could put money in their purses. Thus, towards the end of the eighteenth century a change came about which, if I were rewriting history, I should describe more fully and think of greater importance than the Crusades or the Wars of the Roses. The middle-class woman began to write. For if *Pride and Prejudice* matters, and *Middlemarch* and *Villette* and *Wuthering Heights* matter, then it matters far more than I can prove in an hour's discourse that women generally, and not merely the lonely aristocrat shut up in her country house among her folios and her flatterers, took to writing. Without those forerunners, Jane Austen and the Brontës and George Eliot could no more have written than Shakespeare could have written without Marlowe, or Marlowe without Chaucer, or Chaucer without those

forgotten poets who paved the ways and tamed the natural savagery of the tongue. For masterpieces are not
single and solitary births; they are the outcome of many
years of thinking in common, of thinking by the body
of the people, so that the experience of the mass is behind
the single voice. Jane Austen should have laid a wreath
upon the grave of Fanny Burney, and George Eliot done
homage to the robust shade of Eliza Carter—the valiant
old woman who tied a bell to her bedstead in order that
she might wake early and learn Greek. All women together ought to let flowers fall upon the tomb of Aphra
Behn which is, most scandalously but rather appropri-
ately, in Westminster Abbey, for it was she who earned
them the right to speak their minds. It is she—shady
and amorous as she was—who makes it not quite fantastic for me to say to you tonight: Earn five hundred
a year by your wits.

Here, then, one had reached the early nineteenth century. And here, for the first time, I found several shelves
given up entirely to the works of women. But why, I
could not help asking, as I ran my eyes over them, were
they, with very few exceptions, all novels? The original
impulse was to poetry. The "supreme head of song"
was a poetess. Both in France and in England the
women poets precede the women novelists. Moreover,
I thought, looking at the four famous names, what had
George Eliot in common with Emily Brontë? Did not
Charlotte Brontë fail entirely to understand Jane Austen? Save for the possibly relevant fact that not one of
them had a child, four more incongruous characters
could not have met together in a room—so much so that
it is tempting to invent a meeting and a dialogue between
them. Yet by some strange force they were all compelled,

when they wrote, to write novels. Had it something to do with being born of the middle class, I asked; and with the fact, which Miss Emily Davies a little later was so strikingly to demonstrate, that the middle-class family in the early nineteenth century was possessed only of a single sitting-room between them? If a woman wrote, she would have to write in the common sitting-room. And, as Miss Nightingale was so vehemently to complain,—"women never have an half hour . . . that they can call their own"—she was always interrupted. Still it would be easier to write prose and fiction there than to write poetry or a play. Less concentration is required. Jane Austen wrote like that to the end of her days. "How she was able to effect all this," her nephew writes in his Memoir, "is surprising, for she had no separate study to repair to, and most of the work must have been done in the general sitting-room, subject to all kinds of casual interruptions. She was careful that her occupation should not be suspected by servants or visitors or any persons beyond her own family party."[1] Jane Austen hid her manuscripts or covered them with a piece of blotting-paper. Then, again, all the literary training that a woman had in the early nineteenth century was training in the observation of character, in the analysis of emotion. Her sensibility had been educated for centuries by the influences of the common sitting-room. People's feelings were impressed on her; personal relations were always before her eyes. Therefore, when the middle-class woman took to writing, she naturally wrote novels, even though, as seems evident enough, two of the four famous women here named were not by nature novelists. Emily Brontë should have written poetic plays; the overflow

1 *Memoir of Jane Austen*, by her nephew, James Edward Austen-Leigh.

of George Eliot's capacious mind should have spread itself when the creative impulse was spent upon history or biography. They wrote novels, however; one may even go further, I said, taking *Pride and Prejudice* from the shelf, and say that they wrote good novels. Without boasting or giving pain to the opposite sex, one may say that *Pride and Prejudice* is a good book. At any rate, one would not have been ashamed to have been caught in the act of writing *Pride and Prejudice*. Yet Jane Austen was glad that a hinge creaked, so that she might hide her manuscript before any one came in. To Jane Austen there was something discreditable in writing *Pride and Prejudice*. And, I wondered, would *Pride and Prejudice* have been a better novel if Jane Austen had not thought it necessary to hide her manuscript from visitors? I read a page or two to see; but I could not find any signs that her circumstances had harmed her work in the slightest. That, perhaps, was the chief miracle about it. Here was a woman about the year 1800 writing without hate, without bitterness, without fear, without protest, without preaching. That was how Shakespeare wrote, I thought, looking at *Antony and Cleopatra*; and when people compare Shakespeare and Jane Austen, they may mean that the minds of both had consumed all impediments; and for that reason we do not know Jane Austen and we do not know Shakespeare, and for that reason Jane Austen pervades every word that she wrote, and so does Shakespeare. If Jane Austen suffered in any way from her circumstances it was in the narrowness of life that was imposed upon her. It was impossible for a woman to go about alone. She never travelled; she never drove through London in an omnibus or had luncheon in a shop by herself. But perhaps it was the nature of Jane Austen not to want what she had not. Her gift and her circumstances matched each other completely. But I doubt whether that was true of Charlotte Brontë, I said, opening *Jane Eyre* and laying it beside *Pride and Prejudice*.

I opened it at chapter twelve and my eye was caught by the phrase, "Anybody may blame me who likes." What were they blaming Charlotte Brontë for, I wondered? And I read how Jane Eyre used to go up on to the roof when Mrs. Fairfax was making jellies and looked over the fields at the distant view. And then she longed—and it was for this that they blamed her—that "then I longed for a power of vision which might overpass that limit; which might reach the busy world, towns, regions full of life I had heard of but never seen: that then I desired more of practical experience than I possessed; more of intercourse with my kind, of acquaintance with variety of character than was here within my reach. I valued what was good in Mrs. Fairfax, and what was good in Adèle; but I believed in the existence of other and more vivid kinds of goodness, and what I believed in I wished to behold.

"Who blames me? Many, no doubt, and I shall be called discontented. I could not help it: the restlessness was in my nature; it agitated me to pain sometimes. . . .

"It is vain to say human beings ought to be satisfied with tranquillity: they must have action; and they will make it if they cannot find it. Millions are condemned to a stiller doom than mine, and millions are in silent revolt against their lot. Nobody knows how many rebellions ferment in the masses of life which people earth. Women are supposed to be very calm generally: but women feel just as men feel; they need exercise for their faculties and a field for their efforts as much as their brothers do; they suffer from too rigid a restraint, too absolute a stagnation, precisely as men would suffer; and it is narrow-minded in their more privileged fellow-creatures to say that they ought to confine themselves to making puddings and knitting stockings, to playing on the piano and embroidering bags. It is thoughtless to condemn them, or laugh at them, if they seek to do more or learn more than custom has pronounced necessary for their sex.

"When thus alone I not unfrequently heard Grace Poole's laugh. . . ."

That is an awkward break, I thought. It is upsetting to come upon Grace Poole all of a sudden. The continuity is disturbed. One might say, I continued, laying the book down beside *Pride and Prejudice,* that the woman who wrote those pages had more genius in her than Jane Austen; but if one reads them over and marks that jerk in them, that indignation, one sees that she will never get her genius expressed whole and entire. Her books will be deformed and twisted. She will write in a rage where she should write calmly. She will write foolishly where she should write wisely. She will write of herself where she should write of her characters. She is at war with her lot. How could she help but die young, cramped and thwarted?

One could not but play for a moment with the thought of what might have happened if Charlotte Brontë had possessed say three hundred a year—but the foolish woman sold the copyright of her novels outright for fifteen hundred pounds; had somehow possessed more knowledge of the busy world, and towns and regions full of life; more practical experience, and intercourse with her kind and acquaintance with a variety of character.

In those words she puts her finger exactly not only upon her own defects as a novelist but upon those of her sex at that time. She knew, no one better, how enormously her genius would have profited if it had not spent itself in solitary visions over distant fields; if experience and intercourse and travel had been granted her. But they were not granted; they were withheld; and we must accept the fact that all those good novels, *Villette*, *Emma*, *Wuthering Heights*, *Middlemarch*, were written by women without more experience of life than could enter the house of a respectable clergyman; written too in the common sitting-room of that respectable house and by women so poor that they could not afford to buy more than a few quires of paper at a time upon which to write *Wuthering Heights* or *Jane Eyre*. One of them, it is true, George Eliot, escaped after much tribulation, but only to a secluded villa in St. John's Wood. And there she settled down in the shadow of the world's disapproval. "I wish it to be understood," she wrote, "that I should never invite any one to come and see me who did not ask for the invitation"; for was she not living in sin with a married man and might not the sight of her damage the chastity of Mrs. Smith or whoever it might be that chanced to call? One must submit to the social convention, and be "cut off from what is called the world." At the same time, on the other side of Europe, there was a young man living freely with this gipsy or with that great lady; going to the wars; picking up unhindered and uncensored all that varied experience of human life which served him so splendidly later when he came to write his books. Had Tolstoi lived at the Priory in seclusion with a married lady "cut off from what is called the world," however edifying the moral lesson, he could scarcely, I thought, have written *War and Peace*.

But one could perhaps go a little deeper into the question of novel-writing and the effect of sex upon the novelist. If one shuts one's eyes and thinks of the novel as a whole, it would seem to be a creation owning a certain looking-glass likeness to life, though of course with simplifications and distortions innumerable. At any rate, it is a structure leaving a shape on the mind's eye, built now in squares, now pagoda shaped, now throwing out wings and arcades, now solidly compact and domed like the Cathedral of Saint Sofia at Constantinople. This shape, I thought, thinking back over certain famous novels, starts in one the kind of emotion that is appropriate to it. But that emotion at once blends itself with others, for the "shape" is not made by the relation of stone to stone, but by the relation of human being to human being. Thus a novel starts in us all sorts of antagonistic and opposed emotions. Life conflicts with something that is not life. Hence the difficulty of coming to any agreement about novels, and the immense sway that our private prejudices have upon us. On the one hand, we feel You—John the hero—must live, or I shall be in the depths of despair. On the other, we feel, Alas, John, you must die, because the shape of the book requires it. Life conflicts with something that is not life. Then since life it is in part, we judge it as life. James is the sort of man I most detest, one says. Or, This is a farrago of absurdity. I could never feel anything of the sort myself. The whole structure, it is obvious, thinking back on any famous novel, is one of infinite complexity, because it is thus made up of so many different judgments, of so many different kinds of emotion. The wonder is that any book so composed holds together for more than a year or two, or can possibly mean to the English reader what it means for the Russian or the Chinese. But they do hold together occasionally very remarkably. And what holds them together in these rare instances of survival (I was thinking of *War and Peace*) is something that one calls integrity, though it has nothing to do with paying one's bills or behaving honourably in an emergency. What one means by integrity, in the case of the novelist, is the conviction that he gives one that this is the truth. Yes, one feels, I should never have thought that this could be so; I have never known people behaving like that. But you have convinced me that so it is, so it happens. One holds every phrase, every scene to the light as one reads—for Nature seems, very oddly, to have provided us with an inner light by which to judge of the novelist's integrity or disintegrity. Or perhaps it is rather that Nature, in her most irrational mood, has traced in invisible ink on the walls of the mind a premonition which these great artists confirm; a sketch which only needs to be held to the fire of genius to become visible. When one so exposes it and sees it come to life one exclaims in rapture, But this is what I have always felt and known and desired! And one boils over with excitement, and, shutting the book even with a kind of reverence as if it were something very precious, a stand-by to return to as long as one lives, one puts it back on the shelf, I said, taking *War and Peace* and putting it back in its place. If, on the other hand, these poor sentences that one takes and tests rouse first a quick and eager response with their bright colouring and their dashing gestures but there they stop: something seems to check them in their development: or if they bring to light only a faint scribble in that corner and a blot over there, and nothing appears whole and entire, then one heaves a sigh of disappointment and says, Another failure. This novel has come to grief somewhere.

And for the most part, of course, novels do come to grief somewhere. The imagination falters under the enormous strain. The insight is confused; it can no longer distinguish between the true and the false; it has no longer the strength to go on with the vast labour that calls at every moment for the use of so many different faculties. But how would all this be affected by the sex of the novelist, I wondered, looking at *Jane Eyre* and the others. Would the fact of her sex in any way interfere with the integrity of a woman novelist—that integrity which I take to be the backbone of the writer? Now, in the passages I have quoted from *Jane Eyre,* it is clear that anger was tampering with the integrity of Charlotte Brontë the novelist. She left her story, to which her entire devotion was due, to attend to some personal grievance. She remembered that she had been starved of her proper due of experience—she had been made to stagnate in a parsonage mending stockings when she wanted to wander free over the world. Her imagination swerved from indignation and we feel it swerve. But there were many more influences than anger tugging at her imagination and deflecting it from its path. Ignorance, for instance. The portrait of Rochester is drawn in the dark. We feel the influence of fear in it; just as we constantly feel an acidity which is the result of oppression, a buried suffering smouldering beneath her passion, a rancour which contracts those books, splendid as they are, with a spasm of pain.

And since a novel has this correspondence to real life,

its values are to some extent those of real life. But it is obvious that the values of women differ very often from the values which have been made by the other sex; naturally, this is so. Yet it is the masculine values that prevail. Speaking crudely, football and sport are "important"; the worship of fashion, the buying of clothes "trivial." And these values are inevitably transferred from life to fiction. This is an important book, the critic assumes, because it deals with war. This is an insignificant book because it deals with the feelings of women in a drawing-room. A scene in a battlefield is more important than a scene in a shop—everywhere and much more subtly the difference of value persists. The whole structure, therefore, of the early nineteenth-century novel was raised, if one was a woman, by a mind which was slightly pulled from the straight, and made to alter its clear vision in deference to external authority. One has only to skim those old forgotten novels and listen to the tone of voice in which they are written to divine that the writer was meeting criticism; she was saying this by way of aggression, or that by way of conciliation. She was admitting that she was "only a woman," or protesting that she was "as good as a man." She met that criticism as her temperament dictated, with docility and diffidence, or with anger and emphasis. It does not matter which it was; she was thinking of something other than the thing itself. Down comes her book upon our heads. There was a flaw in the centre of it. And I thought of all the women's novels that lie scattered, like small pock-marked apples in an orchard, about the second-hand book shops of London. It was the flaw in the center that had rotted them. She had altered her values in deference to the opinion of others.

But how impossible it must have been for them not to budge either to the right or to the left. What genius, what integrity it must have required in face of all that criticism, in the midst of that purely patriarchal society, to hold fast to the thing as they saw it without shrinking. Only Jane Austen did it and Emily Brontë. It is another feather, perhaps the finest, in their caps. They wrote as women write, not as men write. Of all the thousand women who wrote novels then, they alone entirely ignored the perpetual admonitions of the eternal pedagogue—write this, think that. They alone were deaf to that persistent voice, now grumbling, now patronising, now domineering, now grieved, now shocked, now angry, now avuncular, that voice which cannot let women alone, but must be at them, like some too conscientious governess, adjuring them, like Sir Egerton Brydges, to be refined; dragging even into the criticism of poetry criticism of sex;[1] admonishing them, if they would be good and win, as I suppose, some shiny prize, to keep within certain limits which the gentleman in question thinks suitable: " . . . female novelists should only aspire to excellence by courageously acknowledging the limitations of their sex."[2] That puts the matter in a nutshell, and when I tell you, rather to your surprise, that this sentence was written not in August 1828 but in August 1928, you will agree, I think, that however delightful it is to us now, it represents a vast body of

1 "[She] has a metaphysical purpose, and that is a dangerous obsession, especially with a woman, for women rarely possess men's healthy love of rhetoric. It is a strange lack in the sex which is in other things more primitive and more materialistic."—*New Criterion*, June 1928.

2 "If, like the reporter, you believe that female novelists should only aspire to excellence by courageously acknowledging the limitations of their sex (Jane Austen [has] demonstrated how gracefully this gesture can be accomplished). . . ."—*Life and Letters*, August 1928.

opinion—I am not going to stir those old pools, I take only what chance has floated to my feet—that was far more vigorous and far more vocal a century ago. It would have needed a very stalwart young woman in 1828 to disregard all those snubs and chidings and promises of prizes. One must have been something of a firebrand to say to oneself, Oh, but they can't buy literature too. Literature is open to everybody. I refuse to allow you, Beadle though you are, to turn me off the grass. Lock up your libraries if you like; but there is no gate, no lock, no bolt that you can set upon the freedom of my mind.

But whatever effect discouragement and criticism had upon their writing—and I believe that they had a very great effect—that was unimportant compared with the other difficulty which faced them (I was still considering those early nineteenth-century novelists) when they came to set their thoughts on paper—that is that they had no tradition behind them, or one so short and partial that it was of little help. For we think back through our mothers if we are women. It is useless to go to the great men writers for help, however much one may go to them for pleasure. Lamb, Browne, Thackeray, Newman, Sterne, Dickens, De Quincey—whoever it may be—never helped a woman yet, though she may have learnt a few tricks of them and adapted them to her use. The weight, the pace, the stride of a man's mind are too unlike her own for her to lift anything substantial from him successfully. The ape is too distant to be sedulous. Perhaps the first thing she would find, setting pen to paper, was that there was no common sentence ready for her use. All the great novelists like Thackeray and Dickens and Balzac have written a natural prose, swift but not slovenly, expressive but not precious, taking their own tint without ceasing to be common property. They have based it on the sentence that was current at the time. The sentence that was current at the beginning of the nineteenth century ran something like this perhaps: "The grandeur of their works was an argument with them, not to stop short, but to proceed. They could have no higher excitement or satisfaction than in the exercise of their art and endless generations of truth and beauty. Success prompts to exertion; and habit facilitates success." That is a man's sentence; behind it one can see Johnson, Gibbon and the rest. It was a sentence that was unsuited for a woman's use. Charlotte Brontë, with all her splendid gift for prose, stumbled and fell with that clumsy weapon in her hands. George Eliot committed atrocities with it that beggar description. Jane Austen looked at it and laughed at it and devised a perfectly natural, shapely sentence proper for her own use and never departed from it. Thus, with less genius for writing than Charlotte Brontë, she got infinitely more said. Indeed, since freedom and fullness of expression are of the essence of the art, such a lack of tradition, such a scarcity and inadequacy of tools, must have told enormously upon the writing of women. Moreover, a book is not made of sentences laid end to end, but of sentences built, if an image helps, into arcades or domes. And this shape too has been made by men out of their own needs for their own uses. There is no reason to think that the form of the epic or of the poetic play suits a woman any more than the sentence suits her. But all the older forms of literature were hardened and set by the time she became a writer. The novel alone was young enough to be soft in her hands—another reason, perhaps, why she wrote novels. Yet who shall say that even now "the novel" (I give it inverted commas to mark my sense of the words' inadequacy), who shall say that even this most pliable of all forms is rightly shaped for her use? No doubt we shall find her knocking that into shape for herself when she has the free use of her limbs; and providing some new vehicle, not necessarily in verse, for the poetry in her. For it is the poetry that is still denied outlet. And I went on to ponder how a woman nowadays would write a poetic tragedy in five acts—would she use verse—would she not use prose rather?

But these are difficult questions which lie in the twilight of the future. I must leave them, if only because they stimulate me to wander from my subject into trackless forests where I shall be lost and, very likely, devoured by wild beasts. I do not want, and I am sure that you do not want me, to broach that very dismal subject, the future of fiction, so that I will only pause here one moment to draw your attention to the great part which must be played in that future so far as women are concerned by physical conditions. The book has somehow to be adapted to the body, and at a venture one would say that women's books should be shorter, more concentrated, than those of men, and framed so that they do not need long hours of steady and uninterrupted work. For interruptions there will always be. Again, the nerves that feed the brain would seem to differ in men and women, and if you are going to make them work their best and hardest, you must find out what treatment suits them—whether these hours of lectures, for instance, which the monks devised, presumably, hundreds of years ago, suit them—what alternations of work and rest they need, interpreting rest not as doing nothing but as doing something but something that is different; and what should that difference be? All this should be discussed and discovered; all this is part of the question of women and fiction. And yet, I continued, approaching the bookcase again, where shall I find that elaborate study of the psychology of women by a woman? If through their incapacity to play football women are not going to be allowed to practise medicine——

Happily my thoughts were now given another turn.

FIVE

I had come at last, in the course of this rambling, to the shelves which hold books by the living; by women and by men; for there are almost as many books written by women now as by men. Or if that is not yet quite true, if the male is still the voluble sex, it is certainly true that women no longer write novels solely. There are Jane Harrison's books on Greek archaeology; Vernon Lee's books on aesthetics; Gertrude Bell's books on Persia. There are books on all sorts of subjects which a generation ago no woman could have touched. There are poems and plays and criticism; there are histories and biographies, books of travel and books of scholarship and research; there are even a few philosophies and books about science and economics. And though novels predominate, novels themselves may very well have changed from association with books of a different feather. The natural simplicity, the epic age of women's writing, may have gone. Reading and criticism may have given her a wider range, a greater subtlety. The impulse towards autobiography may be spent. She may be beginning to use writing as an art, not as a method of self-expression. Among these new novels one might find an answer to several such questions.

I took down one of them at random. It stood at the very end of the shelf, was called *Life's Adventure*, or some such title, by Mary Carmichael, and was published in this very month of October. It seems to be her first book, I said to myself, but one must read it as if it were the last volume in a fairly long series, continuing all those other books that I have been glancing at—Lady Winchilsea's poems and Aphra Behn's plays and the novels of the four great novelists. For books continue each other, in spite of our habit of judging them separately. And I must also consider her—this unknown woman— as the descendant of all those other women whose circumstances I have been glancing at and see what she inherits of their characteristics and restrictions. So, with a sigh, because novels so often provide an anodyne and not an antidote, glide one into torpid slumbers instead of rousing one with a burning brand, I settled down with a notebook and a pencil to make what I could of Mary Carmichael's first novel, *Life's Adventure*.

To begin with, I ran my eye up and down the page. I am going to get the hang of her sentences first, I said, before I load my memory with blue eyes and brown and the relationship that there may be between Chloe and Roger. There will be time for that when I have decided whether she has a pen in her hand or a pickaxe. So I tried a sentence or two on my tongue. Soon it was obvious that something was not quite in order. The smooth gliding of sentence after sentence was interrupted. Something tore, something scratched; a single word here and there flashed its torch in my eyes. She was "unhanding" herself as they say in the old plays. She is like a person striking a match that will not light, I thought. But why, I asked her as if she were present, are Jane Austen's sentences not of the right shape for you? Must they all be scrapped because Emma and Mr. Woodhouse are dead? Alas, I sighed, that it should be so. For while Jane Austen breaks from melody to melody as Mozart from song to song, to read this writing was like being out at sea in an open boat. Up one went, down one sank. This terseness, this short-windedness, might mean that she was afraid of something; afraid of being called "sentimental" perhaps; or she remembers that women's writing has been called flowery and so provides a superfluity of thorns; but until I have read a scene with some care, I cannot be sure whether she is being herself or some one else. At any rate, she does not lower one's vitality, I thought, reading more carefully. But she is heaping up too many facts. She will not be able to use half of them in a book of this size. (It was about half the length of *Jane Eyre*.) However, by some means or other she succeeded in getting us all—Roger, Chloe, Olivia, Tony and Mr. Bigham—in a canoe up the river. Wait a moment, I said, leaning back in my chair, I must consider the whole thing more carefully before I go any further.

I am almost sure, I said to myself, that Mary Carmichael is playing a trick on us. For I feel as one feels on a switchback railway when the car, instead of sinking, as one has been led to expect, swerves up again. Mary is tampering with the expected sequence. First she broke the sentence; now she has broken the sequence. Very

well, she has every right to do both these things if she
does them not for the sake of breaking, but for the sake
of creating. Which of the two it is I cannot be sure until
she has faced herself with a situation. I will give her
every liberty, I said, to choose what that situation shall
be; she shall make it of tin cans and old kettles if she
likes; but she must convince me that she believes it to
be a situation; and then when she has made it she must
face it. She must jump. And, determined to do my duty
by her as reader if she would do her duty by me as
writer, I turned the page and read . . . I am sorry to
break off so abruptly. Are there no men present? Do
you promise me that behind that red curtain over there
the figure of Sir Chartres Biron is not concealed? We are
all women, you assure me? Then I may tell you that
the very next words I read were these—"Chloe liked
Olivia . . ." Do not start. Do not blush. Let us admit
in the privacy of our own society that these things sometimes happen. Sometimes women do like women.

"Chloe liked Olivia," I read. And then it struck me
how immense a change was there. Chloe liked Olivia
perhaps for the first time in literature. Cleopatra did not
like Octavia. And how completely *Antony and Cleopatra* would have been altered had she done so! As it is,
I thought, letting my mind, I am afraid, wander a little
from *Life's Adventure*, the whole thing is simplified,
conventionalised, if one dared say it, absurdly. Cleopatra's only feeling about Octavia is one of jealousy. Is
she taller than I am? How does she do her hair? The
play, perhaps, required no more. But how interesting it
would have been if the relationship between the two
women had been more complicated. All these relationships between women, I thought, rapidly recalling the

splendid gallery of fictitious women, are too simple. So much has been left out, unattempted. And I tried to remember any case in the course of my reading where two women are represented as friends. There is an attempt at it in *Diana of the Crossways*. They are confidantes, of course, in Racine and the Greek tragedies. They are now and then mothers and daughters. But almost without exception they are shown in their relation to men. It was strange to think that all the great women of fiction were, until Jane Austen's day, not only seen by the other sex, but seen only in relation to the other sex. And how small a part of a woman's life is that; and how little can a man know even of that when he observes it through the black or rosy spectacles which sex puts upon his nose. Hence, perhaps, the peculiar nature of woman in fiction; the astonishing extremes of her beauty and horror; her alternations between heavenly goodness and hellish depravity—for so a lover would see her as his love rose or sank, was prosperous or unhappy. This is not so true of the nineteenth-century novelists, of course. Woman becomes much more various and complicated there. Indeed it was the desire to write about women perhaps that led men by degrees to abandon the poetic drama which, with its violence, could make so little use of them, and to devise the novel as a more fitting receptacle. Even so it remains obvious, even in the writing of Proust, that a man is terribly hampered and partial in his knowledge of women, as a woman in her knowledge of men.

Also, I continued, looking down at the page again, it is becoming evident that women, like men, have other interests besides the perennial interests of domesticity. "Chloe liked Olivia. They shared a laboratory together. . . ." I read on and discovered that these two young women were engaged in mincing liver, which is, it seems, a cure for pernicious anaemia: although one of them was married and had—I think I am right in stating—two small children. Now all that, of course, has had to be left out, and thus the splendid portrait of the fictitious woman is much too simple and much too monotonous. Suppose, for instance, that men were only represented in literature as the lovers of women, and were never the friends of men, soldiers, thinkers, dreamers; how few parts in the plays of Shakespeare could be allotted to them; how literature would suffer! We might perhaps have most of Othello; and a good deal of Antony; but no Caesar, no Brutus, no Hamlet, no Lear, no Jaques—literature would be incredibly impoverished, as indeed literature is impoverished beyond our counting by the doors that have been shut upon women. Married against their will, kept in one room, and to one occupation, how could a dramatist give a full or interesting or truthful account of them? Love was the only possible interpreter. The poet was forced to be passionate or bitter, unless indeed he chose to "hate women," which meant more often than not that he was unattractive to them.

Now if Chloe likes Olivia and they share a laboratory, which of itself will make their friendship more varied and lasting because it will be less personal; if Mary Carmichael knows how to write, and I was beginning to enjoy some quality in her style; if she has a room to herself, of which I am not quite sure; if she has five hundred a year of her own—but that remains to be proved—then I think that something of great importance has happened.

For if Chloe likes Olivia and Mary Carmichael knows how to express it she will light a torch in that vast chamber where nobody has yet been. It is all half lights and profound shadows like those serpentine caves where one goes with a candle peering up and down, not knowing where one is stepping. And I began to read the book again, and read how Chloe watched Olivia put a jar on a shelf and say how it was time to go home to her children. That is a sight that has never been seen since the world began, I exclaimed. And I watched too, very curiously. For I wanted to see how Mary Carmichael set to work to catch those unrecorded gestures, those unsaid or half-said words, which form themselves, no more palpably than the shadows of moths on the ceiling, when women are alone, unlit by the capricious and coloured light of the other sex. She will need to hold her breath, I said, reading on, if she is to do it; for women are so suspicious of any interest that has not some obvious motive behind it, so terribly accustomed to concealment and suppression, that they are off at the flicker of an eye turned observingly in their direction. The only way for you to do it, I thought, addressing Mary Carmichael as if she were there, would be to talk of something else, looking steadily out of the window, and thus note, not with a pencil in a notebook, but in the shortest of shorthand, in words that are hardly syllabled yet, what happens when Olivia—this organism that has been under the shadow of the rock these million years—feels the light fall on it, and sees coming her way a piece of strange food—knowledge, adventure, art. And she reaches out for it, I thought, again raising my eyes from the page, and has to devise some entirely new combination of her resources, so highly developed for other purposes, so as to absorb the new into the old without disturbing the infinitely intricate and elaborate balance of the whole.

But, alas, I had done what I had determined not to do; I had slipped unthinkingly into praise of my own sex. "Highly developed"—"infinitely intricate"—such are undeniably terms of praise, and to praise one's own sex is always suspect, often silly; moreover, in this case, how could one justify it? One could not go to the map and say Columbus discovered America and Columbus was a woman; or take an apple and remark, Newton discovered the laws of gravitation and Newton was a woman; or look into the sky and say aeroplanes are flying overhead and aeroplanes were invented by women. There is no mark on the wall to measure the precise height of women. There are no yard measures, neatly divided into the fractions of an inch, that one can lay against the qualities of a good mother or the devotion of a daughter, or the fidelity of a sister, or the capacity of a housekeeper. Few women even now have been graded at the universities; the great trials of the professions, army and navy, trade, politics and diplomacy have hardly tested them. They remain even at this moment almost unclassified. But if I want to know all that a human being can tell me about Sir Hawley Butts, for instance, I have only to open Burke or Debrett and I shall find that he took such and such a degree; owns a hall, has an heir; was a secretary to a Board; represented Great Britain in Canada, and has received a certain number of degrees, offices, medals and other distinctions by which his merits are stamped upon him indelibly. Only Providence can know more about Sir Butts than that.

When, therefore, I say "highly developed," "infinitely intricate," of women, I am unable to verify my words either in Whitaker, Debrett or the University Calendar. In this predicament what can I do? And I looked at the bookcase again. There were the biographies: Johnson and Goethe and Carlyle and Sterne and Cowper and Shelley and Voltaire and Browning and many others. And I began thinking of all those great men who have for one reason or another admired, sought out, lived with, confided in, made love to, written of, trusted in, and shown what can only be described as some need of and dependence upon certain persons of the opposite sex. That all these relationships were absolutely Platonic I would not affirm, and Sir William Joynson Hicks would probably deny. But we should wrong these illustrious men very greatly if we insisted that they got nothing from these alliances but comfort, flattery and the pleasures of the body. What they got, it is obvious, was something that their own sex was unable to supply; and it would not be rash, perhaps, to define it further, without quoting the doubtless rhapsodical words of the poets, as some stimulus, some renewal of creative power which is in the gift only of the opposite sex to bestow. He would open the door of drawing-room or nursery, I thought, and find her among her children perhaps, or with a piece of embroidery on her knee—at any rate, the centre of some different order and system of life, and the contrast between this world and his own, which might be the law courts or the House of Commons, would at once refresh and invigorate; and there would follow, even in the simplest talk, such a natural difference of opinion that the dried ideas in him would be fertilised anew; and the sight of her creating in a different medium from his own would so quicken his creative power that insensibly his sterile mind would begin to plot again, and he would find the phrase or the scene which was lacking when he put on his hat to visit her. Every Johnson has his Thrale, and holds fast to her for some such reasons as these, and when the Thrale marries her Italian music master Johnson goes half mad with rage and disgust, not merely that he will miss his pleasant evenings at Streatham, but that the light of his life will be "as if gone out."

And without being Dr. Johnson or Goethe or Carlyle or Voltaire, one may feel, though very differently from these great men, the nature of this intricacy and the power of this highly developed creative faculty among women. One goes into the room—but the resources of the English language would be much put to the stretch, and whole flights of words would need to wing their way illegitimately into existence before a woman could say what happens when she goes into a room. The rooms differ so completely; they are calm or thunderous; open on to the sea, or, on the contrary, give on to a prison yard; are hung with washing; or alive with opals and silks; are hard as horsehair or soft as feathers—one has only to go into any room in any street for the whole of that extremely complex force of femininity to fly in one's face. How should it be otherwise? For women have sat indoors all these millions of years, so that by this time the very walls are permeated by their creative force, which has, indeed, so overcharged the capacity of bricks and mortar that it must needs harness itself to pens and brushes and business and politics. But this creative power differs greatly from the creative power of men. And one must conclude that it would be a thousand pities if it were hindered or wasted, for it was won by centuries of the most drastic discipline, and there is nothing to take its place. It would be a thousand pities if women wrote like men, or lived like men, or looked like men, for if two sexes are quite inadequate, considering the vastness and variety of the world, how should we manage with one only? Ought not education to bring out and fortify the differences rather than the similarities? For we have too much likeness as it is, and if an explorer should come back and bring word of other sexes looking through the branches of other trees at other skies, nothing would be of greater service to humanity; and we should have the immense pleasure into the bargain of watching Professor X rush for his measuring-rods to prove himself "superior."

Mary Carmichael, I thought, still hovering at a little distance above the page, will have her work cut out for her merely as an observer. I am afraid indeed that she will be tempted to become, what I think the less interesting branch of the species—the naturalist-novelist, and not the contemplative. There are so many new facts for her to observe. She will not need to limit herself any longer to the respectable houses of the upper middle classes. She will go without kindness or condescension, but in the spirit of fellowship into those small, scented rooms where sit the courtesan, the harlot and the lady with the pug dog. There they still sit in the rough and ready-made clothes that the male writer has had perforce to clap upon their shoulders. But Mary Carmichael will have out her scissors and fit them close to every hollow and angle. It will be a curious sight, when it comes, to see these women as they are, but we must wait a little, for Mary Carmichael will still be encumbered with that self-consciousness in the presence of "sin" which is the legacy of our sexual barbarity. She will still wear the shoddy old fetters of class on her feet.

However, the majority of women are neither harlots nor courtesans; nor do they sit clasping pug dogs to dusty velvet all through the summer afternoon. But what do they do then? and there came to my mind's eye one of those long streets somewhere south of the river whose infinite rows are innumerably populated. With the eye of the imagination I saw a very ancient lady crossing the street on the arm of a middle-aged woman, her daughter, perhaps, both so respectably booted and furred that their dressing in the afternoon must be a ritual, and the clothes themselves put away in cupboards with camphor, year after year, throughout the summer months. They cross the road when the lamps are being lit (for the dusk is their favourite hour), as they must have done year after year. The elder is close on eighty; but if one asked her what her life has meant to her, she would say that she remembered the streets lit for the battle of Balaclava, or had heard the guns fire in Hyde Park for the birth of King Edward the Seventh. And if one asked her, longing to pin down the moment with date and season, but what were you doing on the fifth of April 1868, or the second of November 1875, she would look vague and say that she could remember nothing. For all the dinners are cooked; the plates and cups washed; the children set to school and gone out into the world. Nothing remains of it all. All has vanished. No biography or history has a word to say about it. And the novels, without meaning to, inevitably lie.

All these infinitely obscure lives remain to be re-corded, I said, addressing Mary Carmichael as if she were present; and went on in thought through the streets of London feeling in imagination the pressure of dumbness, the accumulation of unrecorded life, whether from the women at the street corners with their arms akimbo, and the rings embedded in their fat swollen fingers, talking with a gesticulation like the swing of Shakespeare's words; or from the violet-sellers and match-sellers and old crones stationed under doorways; or from drifting girls whose faces, like waves in sun and cloud, signal the coming of men and women and the flickering lights of shop windows. All that you will have to explore, I said to Mary Carmichael, holding your torch firm in your hand. Above all, you must illumine your own soul with its profundities and its shallows, and its vanities and its generosities, and say what your beauty means to you or your plainness and what is your relation to the ever-changing and turning world of gloves and shoes and stuffs swaying up and down among the faint scents that come through chemists' bottles down arcades of dress material over a floor of pseudo-marble. For in imagination I had gone into a shop; it was laid with black and white paving; it was hung, astonishingly beautifully, with coloured ribbons. Mary Carmichael might well have a look at that in passing, I thought, for it is a sight that would lend itself to the pen as fittingly as any snowy peak or rocky gorge in the Andes. And there is the girl behind the counter too—I would as soon have her true history as the hundred and fiftieth life of Napoleon or seventieth study of Keats and his use of Miltonic inversion which old Professor Z and his like are now inditing. And then I went on very warily, on the very tips of my toes (so cowardly am I, so afraid of the lash that was once almost laid on my own shoulders), to murmur that she should also learn to laugh, without bitterness, at the vanities—say rather at the peculiarities, for it is a less offensive word—of the other sex. For there is a spot the size of a shilling at the back of the head which one can never see for oneself. It is one of the good offices that sex can discharge for sex—to describe that spot the size of a shilling at the back of the head. Think how much women have profited by the comments of Juvenal; by the criticism of Strindberg. Think with what humanity and brilliancy men, from the earliest ages, have pointed out to women that dark place at the back of the head! And if Mary were very brave and very honest, she would go behind the other sex and tell us what she found there. A true picture of man as a whole can never be painted until a woman has described that spot the size of a shilling. Mr. Woodhouse and Mr. Casaubon are spots of that size and nature. Not of course that any one in their senses would counsel her to hold up to scorn and ridicule of set purpose—literature shows the futility of what is written in that spirit. Be truthful, one would say, and the result is bound to be amazingly interesting. Comedy is bound to be enriched. New facts are bound to be discovered.

However, it was high time to lower my eyes to the page again. It would be better, instead of speculating what Mary Carmichael might write and should write, to see what in fact Mary Carmichael did write. So I began to read again. I remembered that I had certain grievances against her. She had broken up Jane Austen's sentence, and thus given me no chance of pluming myself upon my impeccable taste, my fastidious ear. For it was useless to say, "Yes, yes, this is very nice; but Jane Austen wrote much better than you do," when I had to admit that there was no point of likeness between them. Then she had gone further and broken the sequence—the expected order. Perhaps she had done this unconsciously, merely giving things their natural order, as a woman would, if she wrote like a woman. But the effect was somehow baffling; one could not see a wave heaping itself, a crisis coming round the next corner. Therefore I could not plume myself either upon the depths of my feelings and my profound knowledge of the human heart. For whenever I was about to feel the usual things in the usual places, about love, about death, the annoying creature twitched me away, as if the important point were just a little further on. And thus she made it impossible for me to roll out my sonorous phrases about "elemental feelings," the "common stuff of humanity," "depths of the human heart," and all those other phrases which support us in our belief that, however clever we may be on top, we are very serious, very profound and very humane underneath. She made me feel, on the contrary, that instead of being serious and profound and humane, one might be—and the thought was far less seductive—merely lazy minded and conventional into the bargain.

But I read on, and noted certain other facts. She was no "genius"—that was evident. She had nothing like the love of Nature, the fiery imagination, the wild poetry, the brilliant wit, the brooding wisdom of her great predecessors, Lady Winchilsea, Charlotte Brontë, Emily Brontë, Jane Austen and George Eliot; she could not write with the melody and the dignity of Dorothy Osborne—indeed she was no more than a clever girl whose books will no doubt be pulped by the publishers in ten years' time. But, nevertheless, she had certain advantages which women of far greater gift lacked even half a century ago. Men were no longer to her "the opposing faction"; she need not waste her time railing against them; she need not climb on to the roof and ruin her peace of mind longing for travel, experience and a knowledge of the world and character that were denied her. Fear and hatred were almost gone, or traces of them showed only in a slight exaggeration of the joy of freedom, a tendency to the caustic and satirical, rather than to the romantic, in her treatment of the other sex. Then there could be no doubt that as a novelist she enjoyed some natural advantages of a high order. She had a sensibility that was very wide, eager and free. It responded to an almost imperceptible touch on it. It feasted like a plant newly stood in the air on every sight and sound that came its way. It ranged, too, very subtly and curiously, among almost unknown or unrecorded things; it lighted on small things and showed that perhaps they were not small after all. It brought buried things to light and made one wonder what need there had been to bury them. Awkward though she was and without the unconscious bearing of long descent which makes the least turn of the pen of a Thackeray or a Lamb delightful to the ear, she had—I began to think—mastered the first great lesson; she wrote as a woman, but as a woman who has forgotten that she is a woman, so that her pages were full of that curious sexual quality which comes only when sex is unconscious of itself.

All this was to the good. But no abundance of sensation or fineness of perception would avail unless she could build up out of the fleeting and the personal the lasting edifice which remains unthrown. I had said that I would wait until she faced herself with "a situation."

And I meant by that until she proved by summoning, beckoning and getting together that she was not a skimmer of surfaces merely, but had looked beneath into the depths. Now is the time, she would say to herself at a certain moment, when without doing anything violent I can show the meaning of all this. And she would begin—how unmistakable that quickening is!—beckoning and summoning, and there would rise up in memory, half forgotten, perhaps quite trivial things in other chapters dropped by the way. And she would make their presence felt while some one sewed or smoked a pipe as naturally as possible, and one would feel, as she went on writing, as if one had gone to the top of the world and seen it laid out, very majestically, beneath.

At any rate, she was making the attempt. And as I watched her lengthening out for the test, I saw, but hoped that she did not see, the bishops and the deans, the doctors and the professors, the patriarchs and the pedagogues all at her shouting warning and advice. You can't do this and you shan't do that! Fellows and scholars only allowed on the grass! Ladies not admitted without a letter of introduction! Aspiring and graceful female novelists this way! So they kept at her like the crowd at a fence on the race-course, and it was her trial to take her fence without looking to right or left. If you stop to curse you are lost, I said to her; equally, if you stop to laugh. Hesitate or fumble and you are done for. Think only of the jump, I implored her, as if I had put the whole of my money on her back; and she went over it like a bird. But there was a fence beyond that and a fence beyond that. Whether she had the staying power I was doubtful, for the clapping and the crying were fraying to the nerves. But she did her best. Considering that

Mary Carmichael was no genius, but an unknown girl writing her first novel in a bed-sitting-room, without enough of those desirable things, time, money and idleness, she did not do so badly, I thought.

Give her another hundred years, I concluded, reading the last chapter—people's noses and bare shoulders showed naked against a starry sky, for some one had twitched the curtain in the drawing-room—give her a room of her own and five hundred a year, let her speak her mind and leave out half that she now puts in, and she will write a better book one of these days. She will be a poet, I said, putting *Life's Adventure*, by Mary Carmichael, at the end of the shelf, in another hundred years' time.

Six

Next day the light of the October morning was falling in dusty shafts through the uncurtained windows, and the hum of traffic rose from the street. London then was winding itself up again; the factory was astir; the machines were beginning. It was tempting, after all this reading, to look out of the window and see what London was doing on the morning of the twenty-sixth of October 1928. And what was London doing? Nobody, it seemed, was reading *Antony and Cleopatra*. London was wholly indifferent, it appeared, to Shakespeare's plays. Nobody cared a straw—and I do not blame them—for the future of fiction, the death of poetry or the development by the average woman of a prose style completely expressive of her mind. If opinions upon any of these matters had been chalked on the pavement, nobody would have stooped to read them. The nonchalance of the hurrying feet would have rubbed them out in half an hour. Here came an errand-boy; here a woman with a dog on a lead. The fascination of the London street is that no two people are ever alike; each seems bound on some private affair of his own. There were the business-like, with their little bags; there were the drifters rattling sticks upon area railings; there were affable characters to whom the streets serve for clubroom, hailing men in carts and giving information without being asked for it. Also there were funerals to which men, thus suddenly reminded of the passing of their own bodies, lifted their hats. And then a very distinguished gentleman came slowly down a doorstep and paused to avoid collision with a bustling lady who had, by some means or other, acquired a splendid fur coat and a bunch of Parma violets. They all seemed separate, self-absorbed, on business of their own.

At this moment, as so often happens in London, there was a complete lull and suspension of traffic. Nothing came down the street; nobody passed. A single leaf detached itself from the plane tree at the end of the street, and in that pause and suspension fell. Somehow it was like a signal falling, a signal pointing to a force in things which one had overlooked. It seemed to point to a river, which flowed past, invisibly, round the corner, down the street, and took people and eddied them along, as the stream at Oxbridge had taken the undergraduate in his boat and the dead leaves. Now it was bringing from one side of the street to the other diagonally a girl in patent leather boots, and then a young man in a maroon overcoat; it was also bringing a taxi-cab; and it brought all three together at a point directly beneath my window;

where the taxi stopped; and the girl and the young man stopped; and they got into the taxi; and then the cab glided off as if it were swept on by the current elsewhere.

The sight was ordinary enough; what was strange was the rhythmical order with which my imagination had invested it; and the fact that the ordinary sight of two people getting into a cab had the power to communicate something of their own seeming satisfaction. The sight of two people coming down the street and meeting at the corner seems to ease the mind of some strain, I thought, watching the taxi turn and make off. Perhaps to think, as I had been thinking these two days, of one sex as distinct from the other is an effort. It interferes with the unity of the mind. Now that effort had ceased and that unity had been restored by seeing two people come together and get into a taxi-cab. The mind is certainly a very mysterious organ, I reflected, drawing my head in from the window, about which nothing whatever is known, though we depend upon it so completely. Why do I feel that there are severances and oppositions in the mind, as there are strains from obvious causes on the body? What does one mean by "the unity of the mind," I pondered, for clearly the mind has so great a power of concentrating at any point at any moment that it seems to have no single state of being. It can separate itself from the people in the street, for example, and think of itself as apart from them, at an upper window looking down on them. Or it can think with other people spontaneously, as, for instance, in a crowd waiting to hear some piece of news read out. It can think back through its fathers or through its mothers, as I have said that a woman writing thinks back through her mothers. Again if one is a woman one is often surprised by a sudden splitting off of consciousness, say in walking down Whitehall, when from being the natural inheritor of that civilisation, she becomes, on the contrary, outside of it, alien and critical. Clearly the mind is always altering its focus, and bringing the world into different perspectives. But some of these states of mind seem, even if adopted spontaneously, to be less comfortable than others. In order to keep oneself continuing in them one is unconsciously holding something back, and gradually the repression becomes an effort. But there may be some state of mind in which one could continue without effort because nothing is required to be held back. And this perhaps, I thought, coming in from the window, is one of them. For certainly when I saw the couple get into the taxi-cab the mind felt as if, after being divided, it had come together again in a natural fusion. The obvious reason would be that it is natural for the sexes to cooperate. One has a profound, if irrational, instinct in favour of the theory that the union of man and woman makes for the greatest satisfaction, the most complete happiness. But the sight of the two people getting into the taxi and the satisfaction it gave me made me also ask whether there are two sexes in the mind corresponding to the two sexes in the body, and whether they also require to be united in order to get complete satisfaction and happiness. And I went on amateurishly to sketch a plan of the soul so that in each of us two powers preside, one male, one female; and in the man's brain, the man predominates over the woman, and in the woman's brain, the woman predominates over the man. The normal and comfortable state of being is that when the two live in harmony together, spiritually co-operating. If one is a man, still the woman part of the brain must have effect; and a woman also must have intercourse with the man in her. Coleridge perhaps meant this when he said that a great mind is androgynous. It is when this fusion takes place that the mind is fully fertilised and uses all its faculties. Perhaps a mind that is purely masculine cannot create, any more than a mind that is purely feminine, I thought. But it would be well to test what one meant by man-womanly, and conversely by woman-manly, by pausing and looking at a book or two.

Coleridge certainly did not mean, when he said that a great mind is androgynous, that it is a mind that has any special sympathy with women; a mind that takes up their cause or devotes itself to their interpretation. Perhaps the androgynous mind is less apt to make these distinctions than the single-sexed mind. He meant, perhaps, that the androgynous mind is resonant and porous; that it transmits emotion without impediment; that it is naturally creative, incandescent and undivided. In fact one goes back to Shakespeare's mind as the type of the androgynous, of the man-womanly mind, though it would be impossible to say what Shakespeare thought of women. And if it be true that it is one of the tokens of the fully developed mind that it does not think specially or separately of sex, how much harder it is to attain that condition now than ever before. Here I came to the books by living writers, and there paused and wondered if this fact were not at the root of something that had long puzzled me. No age can ever have been as stridently sex-conscious as our own; those innumerable books by men about women in the British Museum are a proof of it. The Suffrage campaign was no doubt to blame. It must have roused in men an extraordinary desire for self-assertion; it must have made them lay an emphasis upon their own sex and its characteristics which they would not have troubled to think about had they not been challenged. And when one is challenged, even by a few women in black bonnets, one retaliates, if one has never been challenged before, rather excessively. That perhaps accounts for some of the characteristics that I remember to have found here, I thought, taking down a new novel by Mr. A, who is in the prime of life and very well thought of, apparently, by the reviewers. I opened it. Indeed, it was delightful to read a man's writing again. It was so direct, so straightforward after the writing of women. It indicated such freedom of mind, such liberty of person, such confidence in himself. One had a sense of physical well-being in the presence of this well-nourished, well-educated, free mind, which had never been thwarted or opposed, but had had full liberty from birth to stretch itself in whatever way it liked. All this was admirable. But after reading a chapter or two a shadow seemed to lie across the page. It was a straight dark bar, a shadow shaped something like the letter "I." One began dodging this way and that to catch a glimpse of the landscape behind it. Whether that was indeed a tree or a woman walking I was not quite sure. Back one was always hailed to the letter "I." One began to be tired of "I." Not but what this "I" was a most respectable "I"; honest and logical; as hard as a nut, and polished for centuries by good teaching and good feeding. I respect and admire that "I" from the bottom of my heart. But—here I turned a page or two, looking for something or other—the worst of it is that in the shadow of the letter "I" all is shapeless as mist. Is that a tree? No, it is a woman. But . . . she has not a bone in her body, I thought, watching Phoebe, for that was her name, coming across the beach. Then Alan got up and the shadow of Alan at once obliterated Phoebe. For Alan had views and Phoebe was quenched in the flood of his views. And then Alan, I thought, has passions; and here I turned page after page very fast, feeling that the crisis was approaching, and so it was. It took place on the beach under the sun. It was done very openly. It was done very vigorously. Nothing could have been more indecent. But . . . I had said "but" too often. One cannot go on saying "but." One must finish the sentence somehow, I rebuked myself. Shall I finish it, "But—I am bored!" But why was I bored? Partly because of the dominance of the letter "I" and the aridity, which, like the giant beech tree, it casts within its shade. Nothing will grow there. And partly for some more obscure reason. There seemed to be some obstacle, some impediment of Mr. A's mind which blocked the fountain of creative energy and shored it within narrow limits. And remembering the lunch party at Oxbridge, and the cigarette ash and the Manx cat and Tennyson and Christina Rossetti all in a bunch, it seemed possible that the impediment lay there. As he no longer hums under his breath, "There has fallen a splendid tear from the passion-flower at the gate," when Phoebe crosses the beach, and she no longer replies, "My heart is like a singing bird whose nest is in a water'd shoot," when Alan approaches what can he do? Being honest as the day and logical as the sun, there is only one thing he can do. And that he does, to do him justice, over and over (I said, turning the pages) and over again. And that, I added, aware of the awful nature of the confession, seems somehow dull. Shakespeare's indecency uproots a thousand other things in one's mind, and is far from being dull. But Shakespeare does it for pleasure; Mr. A, as the nurses say, does it on purpose. He does it in protest. He is protesting against the equality of the other sex by asserting his own superiority. He is therefore impeded and inhibited and self-conscious as Shakespeare might have been if he too had known Miss Clough and Miss Davies. Doubtless Elizabethan literature would have been very different from what it is if the woman's movement had begun in the sixteenth century and not in the nineteenth.

What, then, it amounts to, if this theory of the two sides of the mind holds good, is that virility has now become self-conscious—men, that is to say, are now writing only with the male side of their brains. It is a mistake for a woman to read them, for she will inevitably look for something that she will not find. It is the power of suggestion that one most misses, I thought, taking Mr. B the critic in my hand and reading, very carefully and very dutifully, his remarks upon the art of poetry. Very able they were, acute and full of learning; but the trouble was, that his feelings no longer communicated; his mind seemed separated into different chambers; not a sound carried from one to the other. Thus, when one takes a sentence of Mr. B into the mind it falls plump to the ground—dead; but when one takes a sentence of Coleridge into the mind, it explodes and gives birth to all kinds of other ideas, and that is the only sort of writing of which one can say that it has the secret of perpetual life.

But whatever the reason may be, it is a fact that one must deplore. For it means—here I had come to rows of books by Mr. Galsworthy and Mr. Kipling—that some of the finest works of our greatest living writers fall upon deaf ears. Do what she will a woman cannot find in them that fountain of perpetual life which the critics assure her is there. It is not only that they celebrate male virtues, enforce male values and describe the world of men; it is that the emotion with which these books are permeated is to a woman incomprehensible. It is coming, it is gathering, it is about to burst on one's head, one begins saying long before the end. That picture will fall on old Jolyon's head; he will die of the shock; the old clerk will speak over him two or three obituary words; and all the swans on the Thames will simultaneously burst out singing. But one will rush away before that happens and hide in the gooseberry bushes, for the emotion which is so deep, so subtle, so symbolical to a man moves a woman to wonder. So with Mr. Kipling's officers who turn their backs; and his Sowers who sow the Seed; and his Men who are alone with their Work; and the Flag—one blushes at all these capital letters as if one had been caught eavesdropping at some purely masculine orgy. The fact is that neither Mr. Galsworthy nor Mr. Kipling has a spark of the woman in him. Thus all their qualities seem to a woman, if one may generalise, crude and immature. They lack suggestive power. And when a book lacks suggestive power, however hard it hits the surface of the mind it cannot penetrate within.

And in that restless mood in which one takes books out and puts them back again without looking at them I began to envisage an age to come of pure, of self-assertive virility, such as the letters of professors (take Sir Walter Raleigh's letters, for instance) seem to forebode, and the rulers of Italy have already brought into being. For one can hardly fail to be impressed in Rome by the sense of unmitigated masculinity; and whatever the value of unmitigated masculinity upon the state, one may question the effect of it upon the art of poetry. At any rate, according to the newspapers, there is a certain anxiety about fiction in Italy. There has been a meeting of academicians whose object it is "to develop the Italian novel." "Men famous by birth, or in finance, industry or the Fascist corporations" came together the other day and discussed the matter, and a telegram was sent to the Duce expressing the hope "that the Fascist era would soon give birth to a poet worthy of it." We may all join in that pious hope, but it is doubtful whether poetry can come out of an incubator. Poetry ought to have a mother as well as a father. The Fascist poem, one may fear, will be a horrid little abortion such as one sees in a glass jar in the museum of some county town. Such monsters never live long, it is said; one has never seen a prodigy of that sort cropping grass in a field. Two heads on one body do not make for length of life.

However, the blame for all this, if one is anxious to lay blame, rests no more upon one sex than upon the other. All seducers and reformers are responsible, Lady Bessborough when she lied to Lord Granville; Miss Davies when she told the truth to Mr. Greg. All who have brought about a state of sex-consciousness are to blame, and it is they who drive me, when I want to stretch my faculties on a book, to seek it in that happy age, before Miss Davies and Miss Clough were born, when the writer used both sides of his mind equally. One must turn back to Shakespeare then, for Shakespeare was androgynous; and so was Keats and Sterne and Cowper and Lamb and Coleridge. Shelley perhaps was sexless. Milton and Ben Jonson had a dash too much of the male in them. So had Wordsworth and Tolstoi. In our time

Proust was wholly androgynous, if not perhaps a little too much of a woman. But that failing is too rare for one to complain of it, since without some mixture of the kind the intellect seems to predominate and the other faculties of the mind harden and become barren. However, I consoled myself with the reflection that this is perhaps a passing phase; much of what I have said in obedience to my promise to give you the course of my thoughts will seem out of date; much of what flames in my eyes will seem dubious to you who have not yet come of age.

Even so, the very first sentence that I would write here, I said, crossing over to the writing-table and taking up the page headed Women and Fiction, is that it is fatal for any one who writes to think of their sex. It is fatal to be a man or woman pure and simple; one must be woman-manly or man-womanly. It is fatal for a woman to lay the least stress on any grievance; to plead even with justice any cause; in any way to speak consciously as a woman. And fatal is no figure of speech; for anything written with that conscious bias is doomed to death. It ceases to be fertilised. Brilliant and effective, powerful and masterly, as it may appear for a day or two, it must wither at nightfall; it cannot grow in the minds of others. Some collaboration has to take place in the mind between the woman and the man before the act of creation can be accomplished. Some marriage of opposites has to be consummated. The whole of the mind must lie wide open if we are to get the sense that the writer is communicating his experience with perfect fullness. There must be freedom and there must be peace. Not a wheel must grate, not a light glimmer. The curtains must be close drawn. The writer, I thought, once his experience is over, must lie back and let his mind celebrate its nuptials in darkness. He must not look or question what is being done. Rather, he must pluck the petals from a rose or watch the swans float calmly down the river. And I saw again the current which took the boat and the undergraduate and the dead leaves; and the taxi took the man and the woman, I thought, seeing them come together across the street, and the current swept them away, I thought, hearing far off the roar of London's traffic, into that tremendous stream.

Here, then, Mary Beton ceases to speak. She has told you how she reached the conclusion—the prosaic conclusion—that it is necessary to have five hundred a year and a room with a lock on the door if you are to write fiction or poetry. She has tried to lay bare the thoughts and impressions that led her to think this. She has asked you to follow her flying into the arms of a Beadle, lunching here, dining there, drawing pictures in the British Museum, taking books from the shelf, looking out of the window. While she has been doing all these things, you no doubt have been observing her failings and foibles and deciding what effect they have had on her opinions. You have been contradicting her and making whatever additions and deductions seem good to you. That is all as it should be, for in a question like this truth is only to be had by laying together many varieties of error. And I will end now in my own person by anticipating two criticisms, so obvious that you can hardly fail to make them.

No opinion has been expressed, you may say, upon the comparative merits of the sexes even as writers. That was done purposely, because, even if the time had come for such a valuation—and it is far more important at the moment to know how much money women had and how many rooms than to theorise about their capacities—even if the time had come I do not believe that gifts, whether of mind or character, can be weighed like sugar and butter, not even in Cambridge, where they are so adept at putting people into classes and fixing caps on their heads and letters after their names. I do not believe that even the Table of Precedency which you will find in Whitaker's *Almanac* represents a final order of values, or that there is any sound reason to suppose that a Commander of the Bath will ultimately walk in to dinner behind a Master in Lunacy. All this pitting of sex against sex, of quality against quality; all this claiming of superiority and imputing of inferiority, belong to the private-school stage of human existence where there are "sides," and it is necessary for one side to beat another side, and of the utmost importance to walk up to a platform and receive from the hands of the Headmaster himself a highly ornamental pot. As people mature they cease to believe in sides or in Headmasters or in highly ornamental pots. At any rate, where books are concerned, it is notoriously difficult to fix labels of merit in such a way that they do not come off. Are not reviews of current literature a perpetual illustration of the difficulty of judgment? "This great book," "this worthless book," the same book is called by both names. Praise and blame alike mean nothing. No, delightful as the pastime of measuring may be, it is the most futile of all occupations, and to submit to the decrees of the measurers the most servile of attitudes. So long as you write what you wish to write, that is all that matters; and whether it matters for ages or only for hours, nobody can say. But to sacrifice a hair of the head of your vision, a shade of its colour, in deference to some Headmaster with a silver pot in his hand or to some professor with a measuring-rod up his sleeve, is the most abject treachery, and the sacrifice of wealth and chastity which used to be said to be the greatest of human disasters, a mere flea-bite in comparison.

Next I think that you may object that in all this I have made too much of the importance of material things. Even allowing a generous margin for symbolism, that five hundred a year stands for the power to contemplate, that a lock on the door means the power to think for oneself, still you may say that the mind should rise above such things; and that great poets have often been poor men. Let me then quote to you the words of your own Professor of Literature, who knows better than I do what goes to the making of a poet. Sir Arthur Quiller-Couch writes:[1]

"What are the great poetical names of the last hundred years or so? Coleridge, Wordsworth, Byron, Shelley, Landor, Keats, Tennyson, Browning, Arnold, Morris, Rossetti, Swinburne—we may stop there. Of these, all but Keats, Browning, Rossetti were University men; and of these three, Keats, who died young, cut off in his prime, was the only one not fairly well to do. It may seem a brutal thing to say, and it is a sad thing to say: but, as a matter of hard fact, the theory that poetical genius bloweth where it listeth, and equally in poor and rich, holds little truth. As a matter of hard fact, nine out of those twelve were University men: which means that somehow or other they procured the means to get the best education England can give. As a matter of hard

1 *The Art of Writing,* by Sir Arthur Quiller-Couch.

fact, of the remaining three you know that Browning was well to do, and I challenge you that, if he had not been well to do, he would no more have attained to write *Saul* or *The Ring and the Book* than Ruskin would have attained to writing *Modern Painters* if his father had not dealt prosperously in business. Rossetti had a small private income; and, moreover, he painted. There remains but Keats; whom Atropos slew young, as she slew John Clare in a mad-house, and James Thomson by the laudanum he took to drug disappointment. These are dreadful facts, but let us face them. It is—however dishonouring to us as a nation—certain that, by some fault in our commonwealth, the poor poet has not in these days, nor has had for two hundred years, a dog's chance. Believe me—and I have spent a great part of ten years in watching some three hundred and twenty elementary schools—we may prate of democracy, but actually, a poor child in England has little more hope than had the son of an Athenian slave to be emancipated into that intellectual freedom of which great writings are born."

Nobody could put the point more plainly. "The poor poet has not in these days, nor has had for two hundred years, a dog's chance . . . a poor child in England has little more hope than had the son of an Athenian slave to be emancipated into that intellectual freedom of which great writings are born." That is it. Intellectual freedom depends upon material things. Poetry depends upon intellectual freedom. And women have always been poor, not for two hundred years merely, but from the beginning of time. Women have had less intellectual freedom than the sons of Athenian slaves. Women, then, have not had a dog's chance of writing poetry. That is why I have laid so much stress on money and a room of one's own. However, thanks to the toils of those obscure women in the past, of whom I wish we knew more, thanks, curiously enough, to two wars, the Crimean which let Florence Nightingale out of her drawing-room, and the European War which opened the doors to the average woman some sixty years later, these evils are in the way to be bettered. Otherwise you would not be here tonight, and your chance of earning five hundred pounds a year, precarious as I am afraid that it still is, would be minute in the extreme.

Still, you may object, why do you attach so much importance to this writing of books by women when, according to you, it requires so much effort, leads perhaps to the murder of one's aunts, will make one almost certainly late for luncheon, and may bring one into very grave disputes with certain very good fellows? My motives, let me admit, are partly selfish. Like most uneducated Englishwomen, I like reading—I like reading books in the bulk. Lately my diet has become a trifle monotonous; history is too much about wars; biography too much about great men; poetry has shown, I think, a tendency to sterility, and fiction—but I have sufficiently exposed my disabilities as a critic of modern fiction and will say no more about it. Therefore I would ask you to write all kinds of books, hesitating at no subject however trivial or however vast. By hook or by crook, I hope that you will possess yourselves of money enough to travel and to idle, to contemplate the future or the past of the world, to dream over books and loiter at street corners and let the line of thought dip deep into the stream. For I am by no means confining you to fiction. If you would please me—and there are thousands like me—you would write books of travel and adventure, and research and scholarship, and history and biography, and criticism and philosophy and science. By so doing you will certainly profit the art of fiction. For books have a way of influencing each other. Fiction will be much the better for standing cheek by jowl with poetry and philosophy. Moreover, if you consider any great figure of the past, like Sappho, like the Lady Murasaki, like Emily Brontë, you will find that she is an inheritor as well as an originator, and has come into existence because women have come to have the habit of writing naturally; so that even as a prelude to poetry such activity on your part would be invaluable.

But when I look back through these notes and criticise my own train of thought as I made them, I find that my motives were not altogether selfish. There runs through these comments and discursions the conviction—or is it the instinct?—that good books are desirable and that good writers, even if they show every variety of human depravity, are still good human beings. Thus when I ask you to write more books I am urging you to do what will be for your good and for the good of the world at large. How to justify this instinct or belief I do not know, for philosophic words, if one has not been educated at a university, are apt to play one false. What is meant by "reality"? It would seem to be something very erratic, very undependable—now to be found in a dusty road, now in a scrap of newspaper in the street, now in a daffodil in the sun. It lights up a group in a room and stamps some casual saying. It overwhelms one walking home beneath the stars and makes the silent world more real than the world of speech—and then there it is again in an omnibus in the uproar of Picadilly. Sometimes, too, it seems to dwell in shapes too far away for us to discern what their nature is. But whatever it touches, it fixes and makes permanent. That is what remains over when the skin of the day has been cast into the hedge; that is what is left of past time and of our loves and hates. Now the writer, as I think, has the chance to live more than other people in the presence of this reality. It is his business to find it and collect it and communicate it to the rest of us. So at least I infer from reading *Lear* or *Emma* or *La Recherche du Temps Perdu*. For the reading of these books seems to perform a curious couching operation on the senses; one sees more intensely afterwards; the world seems bared of its covering and given an intenser life. Those are the enviable people who live at enmity with unreality; and those are the pitiable who are knocked on the head by the thing done without knowing or caring. So that when I ask you to earn money and have a room of your own, I am asking you to live in the presence of reality, an invigorating life, it would appear, whether one can impart it or not.

Here I would stop, but the pressure of convention decrees that every speech must end with a peroration. And a peroration addressed to women should have something, you will agree, particularly exalting and ennobling about it. I should implore you to remember your responsibilities, to be higher, more spiritual; I should remind you how much depends upon you, and what an influence you can exert upon the future. But those exhortations can safely, I think, be left to the other sex, who will put them, and indeed have put them, with far greater eloquence than I can compass. When I rummage in my own mind I find no noble sentiments about being companions and equals and influencing the world to higher ends. I find myself saying briefly and prosaically that it is much more important to be oneself than anything else. Do not dream of influencing other people, I would say, if I knew how to make it sound exalted. Think of things in themselves.

And again I am reminded by dipping into newspapers and novels and biographies that when a woman speaks to women she should have something very unpleasant up her sleeve. Women are hard on women. Women dislike women. Women—but are you not sick to death of the word? I can assure you that I am. Let us agree, then, that a paper read by a woman to women should end with something particularly disagreeable.

But how does it go? What can I think of? The truth is, I often like women. I like their unconventionality. I like their subtlety. I like their anonymity. I like—but I must not run on in this way. That cupboard there,— you say it holds clean table-napkins only; but what if Sir Archibald Bodkin were concealed among them? Let me then adopt a sterner tone. Have I, in the preceding words, conveyed to you sufficiently the warnings and reprobation of mankind? I have told you the very low opinion in which you were held by Mr. Oscar Browning. I have indicated what Napoleon once thought of you and what Mussolini thinks now. Then, in case any of you aspire to fiction, I have copied out for your benefit the advice of the critic about courageously acknowledging the limitations of your sex. I have referred to Professor X and given prominence to his statement that women are intellectually, morally and physically inferior to men. I have handed on all that has come my way without going in search of it, and here is a final warning—from Mr. John Langdon Davies.[1] Mr. John

[1] *A Short History of Women,* by John Langdon Davies.

Langdon Davies warns women "that when children cease to be altogether desirable, women cease to be altogether necessary." I hope you will make a note of it.

How can I further encourage you to go about the business of life? Young women, I would say, and please attend, for the peroration is beginning, you are, in my opinion, disgracefully ignorant. You have never made a discovery of any sort of importance. You have never shaken an empire or led an army into battle. The plays of Shakespeare are not by you, and you have never introduced a barbarous race to the blessings of civilisation. What is your excuse? It is all very well for you to say, pointing to the streets and squares and forests of the globe swarming with black and white and coffee-coloured inhabitants, all busily engaged in traffic and enterprise and love-making, we have had other work on our hands. Without our doing, those seas would be unsailed and those fertile lands a desert. We have borne and bred and washed and taught, perhaps to the age of six or seven years, the one thousand six hundred and twenty-three million human beings who are, according to statistics, at present in existence, and that, allowing that some had help, takes time.

There is truth in what you say—I will not deny it. But at the same time may I remind you that there have been at least two colleges for women in existence in England since the year 1866; that after the year 1880 a married woman was allowed by law to possess her own property; and that in 1919—which is a whole nine years ago—she was given a vote? May I also remind you that the most of the professions have been open to you for close on ten years now? When you reflect upon these immense privileges and the length of time during which they have been enjoyed, and the fact that there must be at this moment some two thousand women capable of earning over five hundred a year in one way or another, you will agree that the excuse of lack of opportunity, training, encouragement, leisure and money no longer holds good. Moreover, the economists are telling us that Mrs. Seton has had too many children. You must, of course, go on bearing children, but, so they say, in twos and threes, not in tens and twelves.

Thus, with some time on your hands and with some book learning in your brains—you have had enough of the other kind, and are sent to college partly, I suspect, to be uneducated—surely you should embark upon another stage of your very long, very laborious and highly obscure career. A thousand pens are ready to suggest what you should do and what effect you will have. My own suggestion is a little fantastic, I admit; I prefer, therefore, to put it in the form of fiction.

I told you in the course of this paper that Shakespeare had a sister; but do not look for her in Sir Sidney Lee's life of the poet. She died young—alas, she never wrote a word. She lies buried where the omnibuses now stop, opposite the Elephant and Castle. Now my belief is that this poet who never wrote a word and was buried at the crossroads still lives. She lives in you and in me, and in many other women who are not here tonight, for they are washing up the dishes and putting the children to bed. But she lives; for great poets do not die; they are continuing presences; they need only the opportunity to walk among us in the flesh. This opportunity, as I think, it is now coming within your power to give her. For my belief is that if we live another century or so—I am talking of the common life which is the real life and not

of the little separate lives which we live as individuals—
and have five hundred a year each of us and rooms of
our own; if we have the habit of freedom and the courage
to write exactly what we think; if we escape a little from
the common sitting-room and see human beings not always in their relation to each other but in relation to
reality; and the sky, too, and the trees or whatever it
may be in themselves; if we look past Milton's bogey,
for no human being should shut out the view; if we face
the fact, for it is a fact, that there is no arm to cling to,
but that we go alone and that our relation is to the world
of reality and not only to the world of men and women,
then the opportunity will come and the dead poet who
was Shakespeare's sister will put on the body which she
has so often laid down. Drawing her life from the lives
of the unknown who were her forerunners, as her
brother did before her, she will be born. As for her
coming without that preparation, without that effort on
our part, without that determination that when she is
born again she shall find it possible to live and write her
poetry, that we cannot expect, for that would be impossible. But I maintain that she would come if we
worked for her, and that so to work, even in poverty
and obscurity, is worth while.

The Snow Queen

Hans Christian Andersen's
The Snow Queen

translated by Eva Le Gallienne

illustrations by Arieh Zeldich

Harper & Row, Publishers

To Mitch Douglas

The Snow Queen
Translation © 1985 by Eva Le Gallienne
Illustrations copyright © by Arieh Zeldich
Printed in the U.S.A. All rights reserved.
Designed by Al Cetta
1 2 3 4 5 6 7 8 9 10
First Edition

Library of Congress Cataloging in Publication Data
Andersen, H. C. (Hans Christian), 1805–1875.
  The snow queen.

  Translation of: Sneedronningen.
  Summary: After the Snow Queen kidnaps her friend Kai,
Gerda embarks on a perilous and magical journey to
search for him.
  1. Children's stories, Danish. [1. Fairy tales]
I. Le Galienne, Eva, 1899–   II. Zeldich, Arieh,
1949–   ill. III. Title.
PZ7.A542Sn 1985   [Fic]   83-47711
ISBN 0-06-023694-9
ISBN 0-06-023695-7 (lib. bdg.)

Contents

HANS CHRISTIAN ANDERSEN was born in Odense, Denmark, in 1805. His father was a shoemaker and his mother was a washerwoman and the family lived in a one-room house. Given little schooling and often teased for his dreamy ways, the boy enriched his poor and often lonely childhood with fantasy and imagination.

When he was fourteen, Hans Christian Andersen went to Copenhagen to make his way in the world. The Royal Theatre accepted him as a singing student, but his voice broke soon after. He tried various other work without success, and over the next few years he often went hungry.

Then he submitted a play to the Royal Theatre. Although they rejected it, the directors were impressed enough with the attempt to provide Andersen with the basic education he

lacked. The schooling, with children much younger than he, proved trying for the young writer, and literary success did not follow any more easily. His first book, a travel diary, was published privately. At last he received a small stipend from the Danish government, which allowed him to travel and learn and write about what interested him.

In 1835 Andersen published his first book of collected fairy tales. Critics, who had praised his plays and poetry, received it scornfully. Wrote Andersen, "I would willingly have discontinued writing them, but they forced themselves from me."

The magic and brilliant stories, both retellings of folktales and creations of his own, have since become great classics of children's—and adult—literature. "The Ugly Duckling," seen by many as a metaphor for Andersen's own life, "The Little Mermaid," "The Princess and the Pea," "The Emperor's New Clothes," "The Night-ingale," "Thumbelina," "The Steadfast Tin

Soldier," and, of course, "The Snow Queen" are some of the best loved.

When Andersen died in 1875, he was known and loved throughout the world. Today, a statue of the Little Mermaid in Copenhagen harbor welcomes visitors to Denmark. A bronze sculpture of the great storyteller with a book open on his lap and a duckling at his feet graces New York City's Central Park.

It All Began
with the
Troll's Mirror

All right, let's begin! When we get to the end of the story we'll know a good deal more than we do now.

It was all the work of a wicked troll, one of the worst. In fact he was the devil himself.

One day he was in a rare good humor, for he had succeeded in making a very special

[1]

mirror. Everything good and beautiful that was reflected in it dwindled to almost nothing, while worthless, ugly things were magnified a thousand times, till they were that much uglier. The most heavenly landscapes looked like cooked spinach, and the nicest people were turned into hideous monsters who stood on their heads and had no stomachs. Their faces were so distorted they were quite unrecognizable. If you happened to have a tiny freckle, it was sure to spread till it covered your nose and most of your mouth.

"Oh, ho, what fun!" cried the devil.

Each time a good, gentle thought passed through a person's mind, an evil grin appeared in the mirror and the devil roared with laughter at his ingenious invention.

At the Troll School—for the devil ran a

troll school—it was reported that a miracle had taken place. Now at last it was possible to see what the world and its inhabitants really looked like. The trolls dragged the mirror everywhere, and soon there wasn't a country or a human being that had not been distorted by it. Then the trolls decided to fly up to heaven with it and make fun of the blessed angels and of Our Lord Himself.

The higher they flew, the more violently the mirror grinned. It grinned so hard they could scarcely keep hold of it. Higher and higher they flew, nearer to God and His angels. The mirror quivered so with fright-ful laughter that it slipped from their grasp and crashed down to earth, where it broke into hundreds of millions of billions of pieces.

And now it caused even greater misery than it had before, for some of the splinters

were so fine—hardly as big as a grain of sand—that they whirled about all over the world, blowing into people's eyes and getting stuck there. And to these unlucky people everything seemed warped and twisted. They could see only the ugly side of things, for each tiny speck of glass had the same devilish power the whole mirror had possessed before it was smashed. In a few cases a splinter found its way into a person's heart, and this was a dreadful thing, for pretty soon their hearts were turned to solid ice.

Some of the pieces were large enough to be used as windowpanes. Best not look at your friends through that kind of window!

Other pieces were made into eyeglasses. But woe betide the people who made use of these glasses! Their vision became warped and their judgment distorted.

The devil was so tickled by all this he nearly split his sides with laughter. And still the specks of glass went whirling through the air.

CHAPTER ONE

About Gerda and Kai

The big city was so overcrowded with houses and people that scarcely anyone had room for even the tiniest garden. They had to content themselves with a few plants in pots. There were nevertheless two children, Gerda and Kai, who shared a garden somewhat larger than a mere flowerpot. They were not brother and sister, but they were so fond of one another, they might just as well have been. Their parents were quite poor,

and they lived in the attics of two adjoining houses. These attics had windows on opposite sides of the gutter that separated one roof from its neighbor.

In front of each window, the parents had placed a large wooden box filled with earth, in which they grew a few vegetables. And they had also planted two little rosebushes, one in each box. Then it occurred to them to place the boxes straight across the gutter, forming a small enclosure between the windows. It was a lovely spot, bordered on either side with hedges of flowers.

The tendrils of the pea plants hung down over the side of the boxes, and the rosebushes sent out long green shoots which twined themselves around the windows and mingled overhead in a regular triumphal arch of flowers and greenery.

The boxes were quite high and Gerda and

Kai knew they must never try to climb up on them, but they were allowed to step outside their windows and sit side by side on their little stools under the rosebushes. Here they spent many happy hours together.

In the winter, this pleasure was denied them, for the windows stayed closed and were covered with ice. But Gerda and Kai warmed pennies on the stove, pressed them against the frozen windowpanes and made two round peepholes. Through each peephole peered a bright, friendly eye.

In the summertime they had only to climb out through the windows to be together, but in the winter they had to run down one long flight of stairs and up another in order to meet.

"Look! The white bees are swarming!" said the old grandmother as she watched the swirling snow.

"Do they have a queen bee too?" asked Kai, for he knew that the real bees always have a queen.

"Of course they have one," said the old grandmother. "You'll find her where the swarm is thickest. She's the biggest bee of all. She never stays quietly on the ground where she falls, but flies straight up into the black cloud. Sometimes on winter nights she flies through the streets of the city peeping in at the windows, and then they freeze up in the most wonderful way, as though they were embroidered with flowers."

"Oh, yes! We've seen that!" exclaimed the children. So they knew that it was true.

"Can the Snow Queen get in here?" asked Gerda.

"Ho, she'd better not try!" cried Kai. "I'd put her on the hot stove and melt her."

The old grandmother stroked his hair and

began another story.

That evening when Kai was in his room getting ready for bed, he climbed onto a chair near the window and peeked out through the peephole. A few flakes of snow were falling and one of them, the largest, settled on the edge of one of the flower boxes. It began to grow larger. It grew and grew and suddenly it turned into a beautiful lady. She wore a white gauze dress sprinkled with millions of star-shaped crystals. She was delicate and beautiful, but she was made of ice—glistening, dazzling ice.

And yet, she was alive. Her eyes shone like clear stars, but there was neither peace nor repose in them. She nodded toward the window and beckoned with her hand. Kai was frightened and jumped down from the chair. Then he thought he saw something like a great bird fly past the window.

The next day was clear and frosty, but it was soon followed by a thaw, and then came the spring! The sun shone, the green leaves unfurled and the swallows began to build their nests. The windows were flung wide open and Gerda and Kai could sit once more in their little garden above the rooftops.

The roses bloomed that summer as they had never bloomed before. Gerda had learned a hymn about roses and the Christ child. She loved it, for it made her think of her own roses. She sang it to Kai, and he joined in:

"In the valley where the roses bloom,
　The Christ child we shall see;
　We shall talk to Him and hear His voice,
　And blessed we shall be!"

They sat hand in hand rejoicing in God's sunshine. What beautiful summer days! What happiness to sit there among the fragrant roses which bloomed that year as though

they would bloom forever.

One day Kai and Gerda sat looking at a book filled with lovely pictures of animals and birds, when suddenly, at the very moment when the clock on the church tower was striking five, Kai cried out, "*Ow!* I felt something prick my heart! And now I've got something in my eye!"

Gerda put her arms around his neck. She made him blink his eye and looked to see if she could see anything. But no, there was nothing there.

"I think it's gone now," Kai said. But it hadn't gone, for it was a speck of glass from the mirror—the Troll's mirror. That horrible mirror that changed everything great and good into something small and ugly— magnified everything bad and evil and exaggerated every fault. Poor Kai! A splinter had also found its way into his heart. He no

longer felt the splinter, but it was there all the same.

"Why are you crying?" he asked. "You look so ugly when you cry. There's nothing the matter with me. Leave me alone!"

Suddenly Kai shouted, "Just look at the rose—it's all worm-eaten! And that one has a crooked stem! I think they're ugly roses, and these boxes they're growing in are ugly, too!"

And he kicked the boxes and tore two roses off the bushes.

"Kai! What are you doing!" cried Gerda. And when he saw how upset she was, he tore off another rose and jumped through the window back to his own room, leaving Gerda alone.

Later on when she brought him the picture book, he ridiculed it and said it was only fit for babies. When the old grandmother

told him a story, he interrupted with rude questions, and at every opportunity he would sneak up behind her, put a pair of glasses on his nose and mimic her. Soon he was imitating all the neighbors. Anything unattractive or peculiar about them he mimicked to perfection.

"How clever!" people said. "That boy has a good head on his shoulders!"

He was even mean enough to tease poor Gerda, who loved him so devotedly. It was all due to the speck of glass lodged in his eye and the splinter that had pierced his heart.

The games he played were quite different from the old ones, which he now considered childish.

One winter day, Kai went out into the driving snow armed with a large magnifying

glass, and caught some of the snowflakes in the fold of his blue overcoat.

"Look at them through the glass, Gerda!" he cried. The glass made each snowflake look much larger. They looked like exquisite flowers, or six-pointed stars. They were a beautiful sight.

"Aren't they remarkable?" said Kai. "So much more interesting than ordinary flowers! And they're flawless, absolutely perfect—until they begin to melt, of course."

A few minutes later he ran out of the house again, wearing heavy gloves and carrying his sled slung over his shoulder. As he passed Gerda he shouted in her ear, "I've got permission to go sledding in the main square, where all the other boys are playing!" And off he went.

The older boys thought it great sport to

hitch their sleds to the big farm wagons that drove through the square. They went for long rides that way. It was the daring thing to do.

Suddenly, a huge white sleigh appeared. The driver was wrapped in a white fur overcoat and wore a pointed white cap. The great sleigh drove around and around the square, and the second time it passed him Kai managed to hitch his little sled to it and was drawn along behind it. The driver went faster and faster, and all of a sudden swept right out of the square into one of the side streets.

Kai tried several times to unhitch his sled, but each time, the driver turned and nodded to him, and it was as though some strange power compelled him to stay where he was.

Soon they were driving out through the town gates. On and on they sped, and by now the snow was so blinding that Kai

couldn't even see his hand before his face. At last he managed to loosen the rope, but it seemed to make no difference. His little sled still remained fastened to the big one, and on they drove like the wind.

Kai began shouting for help, but nobody heard him, and the great sleigh rushed on through the whirling snow. Every now and then it leaped into the air and flew across ditches and over hedges. Kai was really frightened now. He tried to say his prayers, but all he could remember was the multiplication table.

The snowflakes grew larger and larger until they looked like huge white hens. All of a sudden they were swept to one side, and the sleigh stopped. Kai saw that the white coat and cap the driver was wearing were not fur at all. They were made entirely of snow. Then the driver stood up. It was a woman,

tall and slim and dazzlingly white. It was the Snow Queen.

"We've made good time!" she said. "Why! I believe you're cold! Come and snuggle down under my white bearskin." She made him sit beside her in the big sleigh and tucked the fur around him. Kai felt as though he were sinking into a deep snowdrift. "Are you still cold?" she asked and kissed him on the forehead. *Br-r-r!* Her kiss was colder than ice. It seemed to penetrate his heart, which was half turned to ice already.

"I'm dying!" Kai thought. But this feeling only lasted for a moment. In a second he recovered and was filled with such a sense of well-being that the cold no longer bothered him.

"My sled! Don't forget my sled!" was his first thought. Then he noticed it had been fastened to one of the white hens. She flew

along behind them with his sled on her back. The Snow Queen gave Kai another kiss and he immediately forgot all about Gerda and the old grandmother and everyone at home.

"You shan't have any more kisses," said the Snow Queen. "I might kiss you to death!"

Kai looked at her. She was very, very beautiful. She had the brightest, loveliest face imaginable. She no longer seemed to be made of ice as she had that night when she beckoned through the window. As Kai saw her now she seemed quite perfect. And he was not a bit afraid of her. He talked to her quite easily, even boasted about all the things he knew: arithmetic and algebra, the population and area of all the different countries—everything he'd learned at school. She gazed at him and kept on smiling, and it occurred to him that perhaps the things he

knew didn't amount to so very much after all. He stared at the immensity of space as they flew higher and higher through the great black clouds. Below them the storm whined and whistled, as though crooning an old folk song.

They flew over forests and lakes, over oceans and many foreign lands. Far below the icy wind shrieked, the wolves howled and the black crows screeched as they wheeled over the glistening snow.

But high above the earth where Kai and the Snow Queen were flying, the moon shone clear and bright. All through the long, long winter night Kai gazed up at it. When day came, he slept at the Snow Queen's feet.

CHAPTER TWO

The Witch's Flower Garden

Meanwhile, what was happening to Gerda now that Kai had gone away? Where was he? No one seemed to know, no one could give her any news of him.

Some of the boys told Gerda they had seen him hitch his little sled to a large white one which drove into a side street and vanished through the town gates. They had no idea where he could be. Gerda cried her eyes out.

People began saying that Kai must be dead, that he must have fallen into the river

that flowed near the town and drowned.

The days dragged by. It was a long, bleak winter.

Then gradually the sun grew warmer and spring came around again.

"Kai is dead and gone," said Gerda.

"I don't believe it," said the sunshine.

"He's dead and gone," she said to the swallows.

"We don't believe it," they answered, and Gerda didn't really believe it either.

"I shall put on my red shoes," she said to herself one morning, "the ones Kai has never seen, and I'll go down to the river and ask it about him."

It was so very early everyone was still asleep. Gerda put on her new red shoes, kissed the old grandmother, and went all by herself through the town gates and down to the river.

"Is it true that you've taken my Kai from me?" she asked the river. "I'll make you a present of my new red shoes if you'll give him back to me."

It seemed to Gerda that the ripples on the water nodded to her in a mysterious way, so she took off her red shoes—her most precious possession—and threw them into the stream. But they fell quite close to the bank and a little wave soon brought them back and laid them at her feet. It was as though the river refused to accept her present, since it hadn't taken little Kai and couldn't give him back to her.

"Perhaps I didn't throw them far enough," thought Gerda. So she climbed into a boat that lay among the rushes, crept right out onto the prow, and flung the shoes into the water with all her might. The sudden movement loosened the boat from its moorings,

and before Gerda could jump out, it was some way from the bank and was soon drifting rapidly downstream.

Gerda began to cry, she was so frightened. There was no one to hear her, only the sparrows—and they couldn't very well carry her ashore. But they flew along the bank, chirping as though to comfort her, "We're here! We're here!"

Gerda sat quite still in her stockinged feet, watching her little red shoes floating behind the boat as it sped on. They couldn't quite catch up with it. The boat went much too fast for them.

The scenery on both sides of the river was beautiful. The banks were covered with wild flowers. Old trees shaded the green meadows where cows and sheep were grazing, but there was not a single human being to be seen.

"Perhaps the river is taking me to Kai," thought Gerda, and she felt more cheerful. The hours went by and she stood up in the boat gazing at the lovely countryside.

Then, all of a sudden, she saw a tiny house with a thatched roof and little windows of colored glass standing in the center of a large cherry orchard. Two wooden soldiers stood guard outside the door and shouldered arms whenever anyone went by. Gerda, thinking they were real, called out to them, but of course they didn't answer. She was now quite near to them, for the current had swept the boat close in to the shore. She called to them again, this time quite loudly, and out of the tiny house came an old, old woman leaning on a crooked stick. She was wearing a huge sun hat painted all over with the most lovely flowers.

"Why, you poor little child!" cried the old woman. "How do you happen to be drifting down this river, traveling all alone out into the great wide world?" As she spoke she waded out into the deep water, hooked onto the boat with the crook of her stick and pulled it ashore. Then, she lifted Gerda out onto the bank.

Though it was good to be on dry land again, Gerda couldn't help being rather scared of the strange old woman.

"Now, tell me who you are and how you got here," the old woman said. Gerda told her the whole story. As she listened, the old woman kept on nodding her head and muttering, "Hmm! Hmm!"

At last Gerda asked her if she had seen Kai.

"No! I haven't seen him yet," she answered. "But don't you worry, he's sure to be

here presently. Meanwhile, you come and taste my cherries and look at all my pretty flowers. You'll find them more thrilling than any picture book. And, what's more, each one has a marvelous tale to tell!" Then she took Gerda's hand, led her into the little house and shut the door.

The windows were set high up near the ceiling, and the sunlight shining through their red, blue and yellow panes made strange patterns of variegated colors. On the table stood a bowl of the most wonderful cherries.

Gerda was no longer scared, and she ate as many as she liked, while the old woman combed her hair with a fine gold comb. The shiny golden curls framed Gerda's little face, which was as sweet and fresh as a rose.

"I've longed for a dear little girl like you!" said the old woman. "You'll see! We shall get

along splendidly, we two!"

She went on combing Gerda's hair, and gradually Gerda forgot all about Kai, for the old woman was a witch, you see—not a bad witch, though. She only practiced witchcraft now and then, just for the fun of it. She was so anxious to keep Gerda with her that she went out into the garden and pointed her stick at all the rosebushes blooming there. One by one, as she pointed at them, they sank into the earth and disappeared, blooms and all. She was afraid that if Gerda saw them, she might be reminded of Kai and her own roses at home, and try to run away. Then the old woman went back into the house to fetch Gerda and show her around the garden.

How fragrant, how exquisite it was! Gerda had never seen so many flowers. Spring flowers, summer flowers, autumn flowers, all blooming together in the most

incredible profusion. It was much more beautiful than any picture book. Gerda jumped for joy and spent the rest of the day playing among the flowers, till the sun went down behind the cherry trees. Then she was tucked into a soft bed, under a red silk coverlet lined with blue violets. She fell into a deep sleep full of happy dreams, like those of a princess on her wedding day.

Gerda spent many days playing in the garden in the warm sunshine. By now she knew every single flower. Although there were so many, she had a feeling there was one flower that was missing, but she couldn't think which it could be. Then one day she noticed the flowers painted on the old woman's hat. Among them was a rose, and it was the prettiest one of all. The old woman had quite forgotten to take it off her hat when she made the other roses sink into the

ground. That's what comes of not keeping your wits about you!

"Why! There are no roses in this garden!" exclaimed Gerda. And she ran out and searched and searched among the flower beds, but in vain. She was so disappointed that she began to cry, and her hot tears fell right on the very spot where one of the rosebushes lay buried. Her tears moistened the earth, and up sprang the rosebush in full bloom, as lovely and as fragrant as it had been before the old witch cast her spell on it. Gerda put her arms around it and kissed its flowers. Then suddenly she thought of her own roses at home, and remembered Kai.

"Kai! I set out to find Kai!" she cried. "What a lot of time I've wasted! Do you know where he is?" she asked the roses. "Do you believe he's dead and gone?"

"He certainly can't be dead," answered

the roses. "We've just been down under the ground among the dead men, and we didn't see Kai there."

"Thank you! Thank you!" said Gerda, and she went from one flower to another, peering deep into their hearts and asking, "Don't you know where Kai is? Can't you tell me?"

But each flower stood in the sunshine dreaming its own dream, lost in its own story. Gerda listened to a great many of them, but not one of the flowers knew anything of Kai.

What did the tiger lily say?

"*Boom! Boom!* Listen to the drum! Listen to the keening of the women! Listen to the chanting of the priests! The Hindu woman wrapped in her long red robe stands beside her husband's body on the funeral pyre. The flames creep upward ready to devour them both—the living and the dead. But the Hindu

woman's thoughts are with a man in the crowd below, whose eyes burn more fiercely than the flames. They set fire to her heart, as the flames set fire to her body—her body which will soon be burned to ashes. Can the flames of the funeral pyre quench that flame in her heart?"

"I don't understand that at all," said Gerda.

"That is my story," said the tiger lily.

What does the morning glory say?

"An old castle towers above the narrow mountain path. The ivy that covers the thick walls grows all the way up to a balcony on which an exquisite young girl is standing. She leans over the railing and peers far into the distance along the path below. She sighs: 'Ah! Will he never come?'"

"Is it Kai you mean?" asked Gerda.

"I'm only speaking of my own story, my

own dream," answered the morning glory.

What does the little snowdrop say?

"A long narrow board hanging between two ropes under the trees—it's a swing! Two pretty little girls in dresses white as snow, with long green streamers on their hats, sit there swinging. Their big brother stands up in the swing. He steadies himself with his arms around the rope, for he holds a bowl in one hand and a clay pipe in the other. He is blowing bubbles. The bubbles burst. A swinging plank, a vision of iridescent spray—that's my story!"

"That's all very well, and it sounds very pretty," said Gerda, "but you tell it so sadly and you tell me nothing about Kai."

What do the hyacinths have to say?

"Once upon a time there were three lovely sisters, fair and delicate. One had on a red dress, the second wore blue, and the third

was all in white. They danced hand in hand by the silent lake in the bright moonlight. A delicious perfume filled the air, and the maidens vanished into the forest. Then, as the perfume grew heavier and sweeter, three coffins glided from the forest and floated out over the lake. Fireflies hovered round them like little flickering lights. In each coffin lay one of the maidens. Were they dead or only sleeping? The scent of the flowers tells us they are dead, and the funeral bells are tolling."

"You make me so sad!" cried Gerda. "And your scent is so strong, I can't help thinking of those poor dead maidens. Oh, is it true that Kai is dead? The roses have just been down under the ground, and they say 'no!'"

"*Ding, dong!*" tolled the hyacinth bells. "We're not tolling for little Kai, for we

don't know him. We're just singing you our song, the only one we know."

Then Gerda went over to the buttercup, shining so brightly above its glossy green leaves.

"You're such a bright little sun," she said, "surely you can tell me where I can find my playmate?"

And the buttercup lifted its bright little face and looked at her. What was the buttercup's song? Alas! It had nothing to do with Kai either.

"It's no use asking the flowers for help," Gerda said. "They're only interested in their own stories—they can tell me nothing!"

And she tucked up her dress in order to be able to run faster, but a narcissus brushed against her legs as she jumped over it. She stopped and looked down at the graceful

flower. Then she bent over it and asked,
"Perhaps you know something? Have you
anything to tell me?"

What did the narcissus answer?

"I can see myself! I can see myself! How
beautiful I am!" said the narcissus. "And my
scent is so delicious! I can see myself! Yes! I
can see myself!"

"What do I care about that!" said Gerda.
And she ran to the far end of the garden. The
gate was tightly closed, but she pushed and
pulled at the rusty bolt and at last the gate
flew open. Gerda found herself in her bare
feet all alone out in the great wide world.

She glanced back three times as she ran,
but no one seemed to be following her. When
she could run no farther she sat down on a big
rock and looked about her. She was surprised
to see that it was no longer summer, but late
autumn. In the magical garden she hadn't

noticed that, for there were no seasons there. Every kind of flower bloomed at the same time, and the sun was always shining.

"Heavens! What a lot of time I've wasted!" cried Gerda. "It's autumn already. I dare not rest here any longer!" And she got down from her rock, ready to start off again.

Her little feet were so tired and sore. Everything looked cold and bleak. The willows were shrouded in mist, and their falling leaves were yellow and withered. The blackthorn still bore fruit, but it was bitter to the taste and puckered up her mouth.

The great wide world seemed to Gerda a gray and dreary place.

CHAPTER THREE

The Prince and the Princess

After a while Gerda had to sit down and rest again. A large crow came hopping toward her across the snow. He'd been watching her for some time, cocking his head from one side to the other.

"*Caw, caw!*" he said. "*Caw! Caw'day, caw'day!*"

His pronunciation wasn't very good, but he felt kindly toward the little girl and asked her where she was going, and what she was

doing all alone out in the great wide world. Alone! That word Gerda understood only too well. She had come to realize its full meaning. She told Crow the whole story of her life and asked him whether he had happened to see Kai.

Crow nodded thoughtfully and answered, "I might have! I . . . uh—yes! I just might have!"

"Do you really think you have?" cried Gerda, and nearly smothered him with kisses.

"Gently! Gently!" said Crow. "It *might* have been Kai. But if so, he seems to have left you for the Princess."

"Does he live with a princess?" asked Gerda.

"He does indeed! Now just you listen!" said Crow. "It's rather hard for me to speak your language. If only you spoke crow talk!"

"I'm afraid I never learned it," Gerda said. "My grandmother can speak it. She knows

all kinds of dialects. Oh, how I wish I knew it, too!"

"Oh, it doesn't matter," said Crow. "I'll do the best I can—but it won't be very good, I warn you!" Then he went on to tell her what he knew.

"Here in this very kingdom lives a Princess who is famous for her extraordinary wisdom, and it's no wonder! She's read every newspaper in the whole world, and has managed to forget every single word they said. That proves how wise she is! Only the other day, as she was sitting on her throne—and that's not much fun either, so they say!—she found herself singing a little song. It began something like this:

"'Why shouldn't I get married?

"'Oh me, oh my! That's not a bad idea,' she said to herself. 'I think I *will* get married!'

"But she was determined to find a man

who could speak up when he was spoken to, and not just stand there looking superior, for she found that very dull. Her ladies-in-waiting were summoned, and when she told them her decision, they were all delighted. 'Just what *we* had in mind!' they cried. 'An excellent idea!'

"All this is absolutely true. You can take my word for it," said Crow. "I've a tame sweetheart who's allowed inside the palace, and she told me all about it."

This sweetheart was a crow, too, of course.

"The newspapers came out with a border of hearts and flowers entwined with the Princess's initials," Crow continued. "They announced that all good-looking young men were invited to the palace to meet the Princess. And the one who seemed most at home there, and who was the best talker, she would

choose as her husband!

"Yes! Oh yes!" said Crow. "You can take my word for it. It's as true as I'm sitting here.

"The young men arrived in droves. There was a great hullabaloo! But for the first two days nothing happened. They could all talk well enough outside in the street, but as soon as they stepped through the palace gate and saw the guards dressed in silver and the lackeys in gold, and the great rooms all lit up with thousands of lights, they became completely tongue-tied. All they could do when they stood before the Princess on her throne was to repeat the last word of everything she said, which didn't amuse her in the least. You'd have thought they were stuffed dummies!

"Yet they chattered away like magpies as soon as they were out in the street again. There was a line of them all the way from the city gates right up to the palace. I went there

myself just to have a look. They got hungry and thirsty, but nothing was offered them, not even a glass of tepid water! A few had been sensible enough to bring sandwiches, but they took good care not to share them with their neighbors. They thought to themselves, 'Just let him have a hungry look, then the Princess will never choose him!'"

"But Kai—what about Kai?" asked Gerda. "When did he arrive? Was he there with all that crowd?"

"Don't rush me! Don't rush me! We're just coming to him! Well, it wasn't until the third day that this funny little fellow turned up. He didn't come in a carriage, not even on horseback, yet he marched boldly up to the palace gate as if he owned the place. He had bright eyes, just like yours, and beautiful long hair. But his clothes were a bit on the shabby side."

"That was Kai!" cried Gerda joyfully and clapped her hands. "I've found him!"

"He had a little knapsack on his back," said Crow.

"No, no—that must have been his sled," said Gerda. "He had it with him when he left home."

"Might have been," said Crow. "I didn't look at it too closely. Anyway, my sweetheart told me that when he went up the steps to the palace door, he didn't seem a bit impressed by the bodyguards in their silver uniforms or the lackeys in their gold. He nodded to them cheerfully and called out, 'It must be very dull standing on those steps all day. I think I'd rather go inside!' And in he went.

"The great halls were ablaze with lights, and all sorts of grand people—high officials and ambassadors—were scurrying about

barefoot carrying golden salvers. It was enough to strike anyone with awe. His boots squeaked most dreadfully, but he didn't seem to care!"

"It *must* have been Kai!" said Gerda. "He had on new boots, I know. I heard them squeaking up in Granny's room!"

"Oh, yes! They squeaked all right!" said Crow. "But in spite of that he marched up to the Princess as bold as brass. She was seated on a pearl the size of a spinning wheel. And all the ladies-in-waiting with their ladies and their ladies' ladies, and the gentlemen-in-waiting with their gentlemen and their gentlemen's gentlemen—who all had pages—stood grouped around the throne. The farther away from the throne they were, the haughtier they looked. And the footman's servant's servant, who always went about in house slippers, stood in the doorway, and was the

haughtiest of all. It almost made you sick to look at him."

"It sounds awful!" said Gerda. "But Kai won the Princess all the same!"

"If I hadn't been a crow I'd have married her myself, even though I *am* engaged," Crow replied. "My sweetheart told me the boy talked almost as well as I do—when I talk crow talk, I mean. He seemed quite at ease and looked so handsome. He told the Princess he hadn't come to woo her, but only to listen to her wisdom—for he thoroughly approved of that—and she thoroughly approved of him."

"It *was* Kai, there's no doubt of it!" cried Gerda. "He's so clever he can do sums in his head, even fractions! Oh, please, won't you take me to the palace?"

"Hm-m, that's easier said than done," said Crow. "How are we to go about it? I'll take

it up with my tame sweetheart. She'll advise us what to do. But I may as well tell you frankly, they're never going to admit a little girl like you."

"Oh, yes they are!" said Gerda. "When Kai hears I'm there he'll come right out and fetch me."

"Wait for me by that stile," said Crow. Then he waggled his head and flew away.

It was after dark when Crow came back again. *"Caw, caw!"* he said. "My sweetheart sends her best to you. And here's a little bread for you. She sneaked it from the kitchen. They've more than enough there, and you must be hungry. She's afraid you can't possibly get into the palace with those bare feet of yours! The guards in silver and the lackeys in gold would never allow it. But don't cry, we'll get around it somehow. My sweetheart knows of a little back stairway

leading to the bedrooms, and she knows just where they keep the key!"

They went into the park and up the main avenue. One by one the leaves fell from the trees, and one by one the lights went out in the palace. Crow led Gerda to a little back door that stood ajar.

Gerda's heart beat fast with fear and excitement. For some reason she felt guilty, though she was doing nothing wrong. She only wanted to make sure that Kai was really there. It *must* be he! It seemed to her she could already see his bright eyes and his beautiful long hair. She remembered how he used to smile at her when they sat in their little garden on the rooftops. Surely he would be glad to see her, to hear about the long journey she had undertaken for his sake and know how miserable they all were when he disappeared from home. She was filled with

both joy and apprehension.

Now they were on the stairs. A lighted lamp stood on a small table on the landing, and there the tame crow came to meet them. She turned her head from side to side and observed Gerda intently. Gerda, remembering what the old grandmother had taught her, made a little curtsy.

"My fiancé has told me such delightful things about you, my dear young lady," the tame crow said. "Your *vita*—as we call it in the court circles—is indeed extremely touching! If you will carry the lamp, I will lead the way. We're not likely to meet anyone if we go straight along this passage."

"But there's someone following us, I think," said Gerda. And just then something swished past her, and she saw great shadows on the wall, shadows of horses with flying manes and spindly legs, of huntsmen and

ladies and gentlemen on horseback.

"Those are only the dreams," said the crow. "They've come to take their Highnesses' thoughts out hunting. It's just as well, for you will be able to observe them better while they're sleeping. I trust," she continued, giving Gerda a penetrating look, "that should you ever rise to dignities and honor, you will show a suitably grateful heart?"

"That's no way to talk!" said the wild crow.

The first room they passed through had walls covered with rose-colored satin embroidered with flowers. Here the dreams kept rushing by them with such speed that Gerda was unable to see any of the lords and ladies clearly. They passed through many rooms, each one more beautiful than the last. Gerda was quite overcome.

Then, finally, they came to the Princess's bedroom. The ceiling resembled the crown of a large palm tree with fronds of precious crystal. And in the center of the room, suspended from a single golden stem, hung two beds shaped like lilies. The one in which the Princess slept was white. The other one was red, and in this one Gerda hoped to find Kai sleeping. She bent over it, gently brushing aside one of the scarlet petals, and saw the back of a little brown neck. It was Kai—she was almost sure of it!

"Kai!" she cried out joyfully, and held the lamp up higher. The dreams swept around the room on horseback. He woke up, turned his head, and—no! It was not Kai, after all! Though the Prince was young and handsome, it was only the back of his neck that looked like Kai.

Just then the Princess peeped through the

petals of her lily bed to find out what was happening. Poor Gerda burst into tears and told the Princess her whole story, including all the crows had done to help her.

"You poor little thing!" exclaimed the Prince and Princess. Then they praised the crows and said they were not the least bit angry with them. In fact, they would see that they were properly rewarded. But they warned them never to do such a thing again.

"Now!" said the Princess. "Which would you prefer? Your freedom, or an appointment as Court Crows for life, with exclusive rights to all the kitchen scraps?"

The two crows bowed low and said they would prefer the permanent appointment. They were thinking of their old age, you see. As they expressed it, "Security in one's declining years is not to be sneezed at!"

Then the Prince got out of his bed and

allowed Gerda to sleep in it. He couldn't very well do more than that! Gerda folded her hands, and thought, "How good animals and people are!" Then she closed her eyes and fell into a peaceful sleep. The dreams rushed in again, this time in the shape of blessed angels. With them came Kai, seated on his little sled. He smiled at Gerda and nodded happily. But of course it was only a dream, so it vanished as soon as she woke up.

The next day she was dressed from top to toe in silks and velvets. She was invited to stay at the palace and enjoy a life of luxury and ease. But she begged the Princess to let her have a horse and carriage and a pair of good stout boots, so that she could go out into the wide world again and search for Kai until she found him. She was not only given a pair of stout boots but a warm muff as well, and her clothes were simply beautiful.

When she was ready to leave, a brand-new coach made of pure gold, with the arms of the Prince and Princess shining on it like a star, drew up to the door. The coachman, the footmen and the outriders all wore golden crowns. The Prince and Princess themselves helped her into the carriage and wished her Godspeed. The wild crow, who was now married, accompanied her for the first three miles. He sat on the seat beside her, for he hated riding backward.

The other crow stood at the palace gates and waved her wings. She didn't feel like going with them. Since her appointment as Court Crow, she'd had far too much to eat and she had a violent headache.

The inside of the coach was lined with sugar cookies and festooned with candied fruits and ginger nuts.

"Good-bye! Good-bye!" cried the Prince

and Princess. Gerda wept, and Crow wept, too. They kept it up for at least two miles. But the parting with Crow was the saddest thing of all. He flew up into a tree and waved his black wings till he could no longer see the coach, which glittered like a ray of sunlight.

CHAPTER FOUR

The Little Robber Girl

They were now driving through a thick forest. The glittering coach shone like a torch in the darkness. The robbers caught sight of it and were almost blinded by its brightness. This was more than they could bear.

"Gold! It's gold!" they shouted. Then they attacked from all sides, seized the horses, killed the outriders, the coachman and the footmen, and dragged Gerda out of the carriage.

"She's plump and she's pretty! She's been fattened up on nuts!" cried one of the robber women, an old hag with overhanging eyebrows and a long scrubby beard. "A little fatted lamb, she'll make a tasty morsel!"

With that she drew a sharp gleaming knife and brandished it in the most terrifying manner. Suddenly, she let out a piercing shriek and dropped the knife. Her own daughter, who was riding on her back, had bitten her on the ear. She was the wildest, naughtiest child you could ever hope to see.

"You loathsome brat!" yelled the mother. For the moment Gerda's life was saved.

"I want her to stay here and play with me!" said the little robber girl. "I'll let her share my bed, but I want that muff and that pretty dress of hers—she'll have to give me those!" Then she bit her mother again so hard that the old hag jumped up and down and ran

around in circles. The robbers roared with laughter. "Look at the old bear dancing with her cub!" they shouted.

"I want to ride in the coach!" said the robber girl. She always insisted on having her own way, for she was spoiled to death and stubborn as a mule. So she and Gerda got in, and the coach went lurching over the rough, unbroken ground, through briars and bushes, right into the very center of the forest.

The robber girl was the same size as Gerda, but much stronger. She was dark skinned and broad shouldered, and her coal-black eyes had something almost sad about them. She put her arm around Gerda's waist and said, "They won't kill you as long as I don't get cross with you! You must surely be a princess?"

"No, I'm not," said Gerda. Then she told the robber girl everything, every single thing

she had been through, and how fond she was of Kai.

The robber girl looked at her solemnly, gave a little nod and said, "I won't let them kill you, even if I *do* get cross with you, for then I shall probably do it myself!"

Then she dried Gerda's tears, took her muff away from her and plunged both hands into its warm furry depths.

The coach stopped at last in the courtyard of an old robber castle. Its crumbling walls were full of great gaps, out of which flew crows and ravens. Huge bulldogs, that looked as though they could devour you in one gulp, leaped about the courtyard. They made no sound, for barking was forbidden.

In the vast hall, which smelled of soot, a big fire burned in the middle of the stone floor. There was no chimney, so the smoke hung in great clouds among the rafters and

had to find a way out as best it could. A large cauldron of soup steamed over the fire, and rabbits and hares were turning on a spit.

"Tonight you shall sleep with me and all my pets," said the robber girl.

After they'd had something to eat and drink, they went over to a corner where some straw and blankets were spread out on the floor. Nearly a hundred pigeons were roosting on the beams and rafters overhead. They stirred in their sleep as the two little girls approached.

"These are all mine!" exclaimed the robber girl, seizing the nearest bird by the legs and shaking it till its wings flapped. "Kiss it!" she shouted, thrusting it in Gerda's face.

Then she pointed to a hole high up in the wall across which some wire netting had been stretched to form a cage. "D'you see

those two up there? They're a pair of ruffians, they are! They're so wild they'd fly right back into the woods if I didn't keep them behind bars!

"And here's my dear old Moo!" she said, dragging forward a reindeer by its horns. It had a shiny copper ring round its neck by which it was kept tied. "He'd escape, too, if he wasn't chained. Every evening I tickle his neck with my sharp knife. It gives him such a fright! Look! I'll show you!" And she took a long knife from a crack in the wall and drew it lightly across the reindeer's neck. The poor beast plunged and kicked with terror. The robber girl gave a shout of laughter and pulled Gerda down on the bed beside her.

"Must you keep that knife with you while you sleep?" asked Gerda rather anxiously.

"I always sleep with my knife handy," said the robber girl. "You never know when you

might need it. Now tell me all about Kai again, and why you went out into the great wide world."

So Gerda told her story all over again, and the wood pigeons cooed softly in their cage while all the other pigeons slept. The robber girl flung her arm around Gerda's neck and, holding her knife clasped in her other hand, was soon—judging by her loud snores— unmistakably asleep.

Gerda, however, didn't dare close her eyes, for she didn't know whether she was to live or die. The robbers sprawled around the fire, drinking and singing, while the old robber hag turned somersaults.

"*Coo! Coo!*" said the wood pigeons, "We've seen your little Kai. A white hen was carrying his sled while he rode in the great sleigh with the Snow Queen. They glided swiftly by, just above the treetops, and

as they passed our nest, the Snow Queen breathed down on us, and all the other fledglings froze to death. Only we two survived. *Coo! coo!*"

"What are you saying up there?" cried Gerda. "What more do you know? Where was the Snow Queen going?"

"Most likely to Lapland, where there's plenty of ice and snow. Ask the poor reindeer in his chains down there."

"Yes! There's always ice and snow in Lapland—it's a glorious country!" said the reindeer. "To be free! To go bounding through those vast glittering valleys! But the Snow Queen doesn't live there. She only goes there in the summers. Her real castle is on an island far up by the North Pole. They call it Spitzbergen."

"Oh, poor Kai!" sighed Gerda.

"Keep still, can't you!" said the robber

girl. "Unless you want my knife between your ribs!"

The next morning when Gerda told her what the wood pigeons had said, the robber girl listened intently, nodded her head, and exclaimed, "Good! That's very good!"

Then she turned to the reindeer and asked, "Do you know where Lapland is?"

"If *I* don't know, who does?" answered the reindeer, his eyes sparkling. "I was born and bred there. Those snowfields were my playground!"

"Now, listen!" said the robber girl to Gerda. "The men are all out, as you see. My old woman's here. We can't get rid of her, but later on she'll have a drink from that big bottle, and after that she always takes a snooze. When that happens, I'll do something to help you!"

She jumped out of bed, flung herself on her

mother's neck, pulled her by the beard and cried, "My own darling nanny goat, good morning!" Then the mother pinched her daughter's nose till it was scarlet. All this, of course, out of pure love.

As soon as her mother had had her drink from the big bottle and had settled down for her snooze, the robber girl went up to the reindeer and said, "I shall miss tickling you with my sharp knife, because you're so funny when I do it and it makes me laugh! But never mind. I'm going to untie your rope and set you free so you can go back to Lapland. But you must promise to take this little girl to find her playmate in the Snow Queen's castle. I'm sure you overheard her story, for she talked very loud and, anyway, you have long ears!"

The reindeer pranced with joy. The robber girl lifted Gerda up and tied her firmly to the

reindeer's back. She even gave her a little pillow to sit on, which was very thoughtful of her.

"There! That's fine!" she said. "Here are your fur boots. You'd better put them on, it'll be cold. But I'm going to keep the muff. I can't bear to part with that. Instead, I'll give you my mother's mittens. They'll keep you warm enough. They're so big they'll come up to your elbows. Here! Put them on! Now your hands look just like my horrible old mother's!"

Gerda wept for joy.

"Stop that sniveling!" said the robber girl. "You should be happy! I don't want you to starve, so here are two loaves of bread and a ham."

These she tied to the reindeer's back as well. Then she opened the door, and after locking up the dogs, she cut the rope with her

knife and said to the reindeer, "Off you go! And mind you take good care of her!"

Gerda stretched out her hands in their huge mittens toward the robber girl and said good-bye.

The reindeer dashed away through the dense forest, leaping over stumps and bushes, crossing swamps and speeding over moors. The wolves howled and the ravens croaked. The sky was red, and there was a sound like fireworks exploding overhead. It was as though the heavens were spitting fire.

"Those are my dear old Northern Lights," said the reindeer. "Look at them flashing!"

And he ran even faster than before—through the days and through the nights. The two loaves were eaten up, and all the ham, and suddenly, there they were—in Lapland!

CHAPTER FIVE

The Lapp Woman and the Finn Woman

They stopped in front of a tiny hut. It was a wretched little place. The roof sloped right down to the ground, and the door was so low that the people who lived there had to crawl in and out on their hands and knees. There was nobody home but an old Lapp Woman who was frying fish over an oil stove. The reindeer told her Gerda's story, but he began by telling her his own, which seemed to him much more important. Gerda was so numb

with cold, she couldn't say a word.

"Oh, you poor things!" said the Lapp Woman. "You've still got a long way to go! You'll have to travel well over a hundred miles into the farthest reaches of the Finnmark. That's where the Snow Queen lives. Her blue lights shine out every evening. I'll give you a note to the Finn Woman up there—she can advise you better than I can. I have no paper, but I'll scribble a few words on a bit of dried codfish."

As soon as Gerda had thawed out a little, the woman gave her something to eat and drink. Then she wrote her note on the dried codfish, told Gerda to guard it carefully, tied her once more to the reindeer's back, and off they went.

Again there was a sound like exploding fireworks overhead, and beautiful blue Northern Lights flashed all night long.

At last they reached the Finnmark and came to the Finn Woman's hut. There was no door to be seen, so they knocked on the chimney.

The Finn Woman was small and very grubby. It was so hot inside her hut that she wore practically nothing. She immediately loosened Gerda's clothes and took off her boots and mittens so that she wouldn't be stifled by the heat. Then she put a piece of ice on the reindeer's head and settled down to read what was written on the codfish. She read it over three times till she knew it by heart and then, because it was edible, she popped the fish into the soup kettle. She didn't believe in wasting things.

The reindeer told his own story first and then Gerda's. The Finn Woman blinked her sharp, clever eyes but remained silent.

"You're so wise," said the reindeer. "I've

heard you can tie up all the winds of the world with a little bit of thread. If the skipper unties the first knot, he gets a fair wind. It blows hard if he unties the second. But let him untie the third and fourth and a gale breaks loose that will level a forest. Haven't you a potion this little girl could drink that would give her the strength of twelve men and help her to conquer the Snow Queen?"

"The strength of twelve men, eh?" said the Finn Woman. "Much good that would do!"

Then she went over to a shelf and took down a large roll of parchment covered with numbers and strange hieroglyphics. She studied it so intently that the sweat poured from her brow like hailstones.

Once again the reindeer begged her to help Gerda, and Gerda gazed at her with pleading eyes full of tears. The Finn Woman

blinked again, drew the reindeer into a corner of the hut, and whispered in his ear while she put a fresh piece of ice on his head.

"It's true that Kai is with the Snow Queen. He's quite content there. In fact, he thinks himself most fortunate. But that's all due to the Troll's mirror. He has a splinter of it in his heart, and a speck of it in his eye, too. These must come out or he will never be human again, and the Snow Queen will keep him in her power."

"But isn't there something Gerda could take that would give her the power to overcome all this?"

"She already has more power than I could ever give her," answered the Finn Woman. "Can't you see how strong she is? How do you suppose she's managed to make her way, barefoot and alone, out in the great wide world? Why should people and animals

feel compelled to serve her? She doesn't know she has this power and—and she mustn't learn of it from us. It is the power of a sweet, innocent child. It lies deep in her heart. Somehow she will have to reach the Snow Queen and find a way to rid little Kai of the speck in his eye and the splinter in his heart. And she must do it all alone. There's nothing we can do to help her.

"Two miles from here you will come to the outposts of the Snow Queen's garden. You'll see a large bush growing in the snow covered with red berries. That's where you must leave the little girl. And mind you don't stay gossiping, but hurry back!"

With that the Finn Woman lifted Gerda onto the reindeer, and he set off with all speed.

"My boots! My mittens! I've left them behind!" cried Gerda as the cold pierced

through her. But the reindeer didn't dare to stop. He ran straight on till he came to the large bush covered with red berries. There he set Gerda down, kissed her on the mouth while great tears coursed down his cheeks. Then he turned and hurried back to the Finn Woman's hut.

Gerda was left shivering, with bare hands and bare feet, alone in the icy wastes of the Finnmark. She ran on as fast as she could. A whole regiment of snowflakes came to meet her. They were not falling from the sky, which was quite clear and blazing with Northern Lights. They were skimming along the ground, and the nearer they came, the larger they grew. Gerda remembered how big and strange they had looked when she saw them through the magnifying glass at home, but these were even bigger and much more terrifying, for these were alive. They

were the Snow Queen's vanguard. Some of them were shaped like huge, ugly porcupines, others like bundles of snakes darting their heads in all directions, others again like small, fat bears with bristling fur. All were dazzlingly white, all were horribly alive.

"Our Father who art in Heaven . . ." Gerda began to pray.

It was so bitterly cold she could see her own breath. It looked like a cloud of smoke coming out of her mouth, and the cloud became denser and denser and was transformed into hundreds of tiny angels wearing helmets and armed with spears and shields.

They grew larger as they touched the ground. More and more of them appeared, and by the time Gerda had finished her prayer, she was surrounded by a whole legion of shiny angels. They pierced the hideous snowflakes with their spears, hacked

them into a thousand pieces and Gerda was
able to go on her way secure and unafraid.
The angels rubbed her hands and feet so that
she no longer felt the cold, and she hurried on
toward the Snow Queen's castle.

Meanwhile, what was happening to Kai?
What was he doing? He certainly was not
thinking of little Gerda, nor did he suspect
that she was there, standing just outside the
castle walls.

CHAPTER SIX

The Snow Queen's Castle
and
What Happened Later

The walls of the Snow Queen's castle were made of drifting snow, and the doors and windows of piercing winds. Inside, the snowdrifts formed more than a hundred rooms, the biggest one stretching on for miles, and all were brilliantly lit by the dazzling Northern Lights. There was never any gaiety in these vast, empty, ice-cold, glittering halls.

No balls were ever given there, not even a small informal dance, where an orchestra of

howling winds could play while the polar bears pranced on their hind legs and displayed their exquisite manners. There were never any parties with lively games of Slap-A-Jaw or Paw-Me-Not. No young lady foxes, all in white, ever gathered there to gossip over a cup of tea. Vast, empty and ice-cold was the Snow Queen's castle.

The Northern Lights blazed on and off so regularly, you could tell the time by them. There was a frozen lake in the middle of the empty, endless hall of snow. The ice on its surface had cracked into a thousand pieces, each piece so exactly like the other, you'd have thought it was some strange work of art. And in the center of this frozen lake sat the Snow Queen—when she was at home. She used to say she was sitting in the center of the one and only valuable mirror in the world, the Mirror of Reason.

Little Kai was so blue with cold that he was almost black. But he didn't notice it, for his heart was practically a solid lump of ice, and the Snow Queen had kissed away any remaining sense of chill. He was busily arranging some flat, sharp slabs of ice, trying to fit them together to form a pattern, as we sometimes try to fit little pieces of wood together, in what we call a jigsaw puzzle.

Kai was completely concentrated on his game. It was called the Game of Cold Reason. Some of the patterns he created were immensely intricate. They seemed to him remarkable and incredibly important. This, of course, was due to the speck of glass imbedded in his eye. Some of the patterns took the shape of words, but he could never succeed in forming the one word he had in mind—the word *eternity*.

The Snow Queen had said to him, "If you

can form that word for me, I will give you the whole world. And you shall have your freedom and a pair of new skates as well."

But even so, he couldn't do it.

"I must rush off to visit the warm countries," said the Snow Queen. "It's high time I had a look at those old black smoke pots!" She meant Etna and Vesuvius, the two volcanoes. "I think I'll whiten them up a bit. It'll do them good. It'll be good for the lemons and grapes, too!"

So the Snow Queen flew off, leaving Kai all alone in the vast, endless, empty hall. He stared at the slabs of ice and thought and thought till his brains creaked. He sat there so stiff and still, you'd have thought he'd been frozen to death.

Just then Gerda came into the castle through the gate of the piercing winds. But when she said her evening prayers, the winds

immediately lay down and prepared to go to sleep. So she was able to walk on into the vast, empty, ice-cold hall. Then she saw Kai. She rushed toward him, flung her arms around his neck, held him tight and cried out, "Kai! Darling Kai! At last I've found you!"

But Kai didn't move. He just sat there stiff and cold.

Then Gerda started to cry, and her warm tears fell on his breast and found their way into his heart. The ice around his heart melted away and the splinter from the evil mirror was dissolved. He looked up at Gerda and she began to sing:

"In the valley where the roses bloom,
    The Christ child we shall see. . . ."

Kai burst into tears! And he cried so hard, his tears washed the speck of glass right out of his eye. He suddenly recognized her and

exclaimed joyfully, "Gerda! Darling Gerda! Where have you been all this time? And where have I been?"

He looked around him. "How cold it is here, how vast and empty!"

And he clung to Gerda, who laughed and wept for joy. Their happiness was so wonderful to see that even the slabs of ice danced with delight, and when they grew tired, they lay down and formed the exact word the Snow Queen had told Kai he must find—the word *eternity*. Now she would have to give him the whole world and his freedom and a new pair of skates as well.

Gerda kissed Kai's cheeks, and they grew rosy again. She kissed his eyes, and they shone like hers. She kissed his hands and feet, and he was once more strong and well. Let the Snow Queen come home whenever she liked—Kai was free! There lay his reprieve,

blazoned in letters of glistening ice!

Kai and Gerda walked out of the great castle hand in hand. They talked of dear old grandmother and of the roses in their rooftop garden. Wherever they went, the winds were still and the sun came out to greet them. When they got to the bush with the red berries they found the reindeer waiting. He had brought a young doe with him, and she gave them her warm milk to drink and kissed them on the mouth.

The two children rode the reindeers' backs, first to the Finn Woman's hut—where they warmed themselves and were given directions for their journey home—then on to the Lapp Woman, who had made them new clothes and had her old sleigh ready for them.

The reindeer and the young doe ran beside the sleigh until they reached the border.

Here Kai and Gerda said good-bye to the Lapp Woman and the reindeer. "Good-bye! Good-bye!" they cried.

The first green shoots were springing up and the first little birds began to twitter. The trees were all in bud, and out of the forest, mounted on a splendid horse which Gerda recognized (it had been harnessed to the golden coach), came a young girl wearing a red cap and with a brace of pistols at her belt. It was the robber girl. She had gotten tired of staying at home and had decided to go traveling. She planned to have a look at the northern countries first, and if she didn't like them she could always set off in the opposite direction. She recognized Gerda at once, and Gerda recognized her. It was a happy meeting.

"A fine friend *you* are, disappearing like that!" she said to Kai. "Making people run

to the ends of the world for your sake! Ha! I can't help wondering if you're really worth it!"

But Gerda patted her on the cheek and asked after the Prince and Princess.

"They've gone abroad to foreign lands," said the robber girl.

"And what about Crow?" asked Gerda.

"Crow is dead," replied the robber girl. "The tame crow is now a widow and wears a bit of black wool around her leg. She pretends to be heartbroken. It's all a pose, of course! But I want to know all that's happened to you! Tell me how you managed to find him!"

So Kai and Gerda told her the whole story.

"And a snip-snap-snorum, high-cock-alorum! I must be off!" cried the robber girl. Then she shook hands with them, promised

to visit them if she should ever be passing through their town, and rode away into the great wide world.

Kai and Gerda walked on hand in hand. It was springtime wherever they went. The trees were covered with fresh green leaves, and the scent of flowers filled the air. They heard the church bells ringing and recognized the high towers of the big town that was their home. They went straight to the old grandmother's door, ran up the stairs and into her room. Here everything was exactly as they remembered it. Nothing had changed. The old clock said *tick-tock* as its hands went round, marking the hour. But as they passed through the doorway, they suddenly realized they were no longer children. They had grown up.

The roses from their rooftop garden peeped in at the open window, and their two

little stools stood out there as before. Kai and Gerda sat down on them and held each other by the hand. The cold, empty splendor of the Snow Queen's castle faded from their minds like an evil dream. Grandmother sat in God's glorious sunshine reading aloud from her Bible. "Except ye become as little children, ye shall not enter the Kingdom of Heaven."

Kai and Gerda looked into each other's eyes and, all of a sudden, the meaning of the old hymn became clear to them:

"In the valley where the roses bloom,
   The Christ child we shall see...."

They sat there, the two of them—grown up, but children still. Children at heart. And it was summer. Warm, golden summer.

THE END

EVA LE GALLIENNE is known and respected throughout the world of dramatic arts and publishing as a performer, director, translator and author. She has translated and adapted numerous plays, including seven plays by Henrik Ibsen, and has appeared in plays by Ibsen, Shakespeare and many contemporary dramatists. A founder and director of the Civic Repertory Company and a founder of the American Repertory Theater, she has received many awards and degrees for her work in the arts.

Among her translations for children, Le Gallienne numbers some of Hans Christian Andersen's most beloved stories, such as "The Nightingale" and "The Little Mermaid." She has also written two autobiographical books, AT 33 and WITH A QUIET HEART, and a picture book for children, FLOSSIE AND BOSSIE.

Le Gallienne was born in London and educated in Paris. Her father was an editor and poet and her mother a Danish journalist, who remembered sitting on Hans Christian Andersen's lap

when he visited her classroom and told stories.

Eva Le Gallienne now lives in Weston, Connecticut.

ARIEH ZELDICH, artist and illustrator, was born in Kiev, U.S.S.R., and graduated from the Ukrainian Polygraphic Institute. His art has been in many exhibits, including a one-man show at the Jerusalem Artists House in Israel in 1975, the Israeli Artists Show in Brussels in 1977, the Art et Amicitae Gallery in Amsterdam in 1978 and the Original Art Show in New York City in 1981–1982.

Mr. Zeldich has illustrated books published in the Soviet Union, as well as the United States. His previous books for Harper & Row include the moving NANA by Lyn Littlefield Hoopes and the vibrant THE MERRY STARLINGS by Samuel Marshak and D. Harms.

Mr. Zeldich now lives in Teaneck, New Jersey.